D1305962

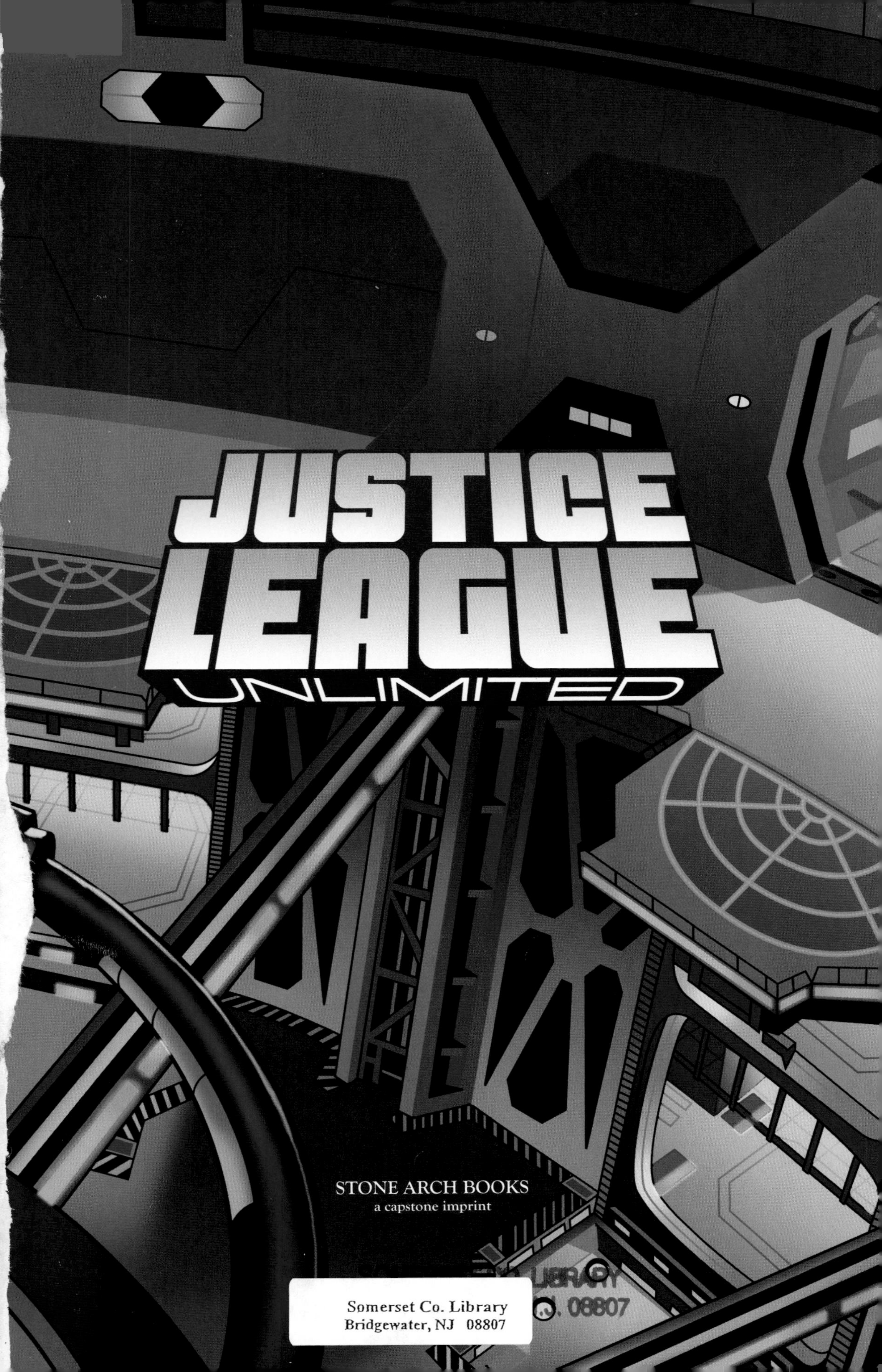

JUSTICE LEAGUE UNLIMITED

STONE ARCH BOOKS
a capstone imprint

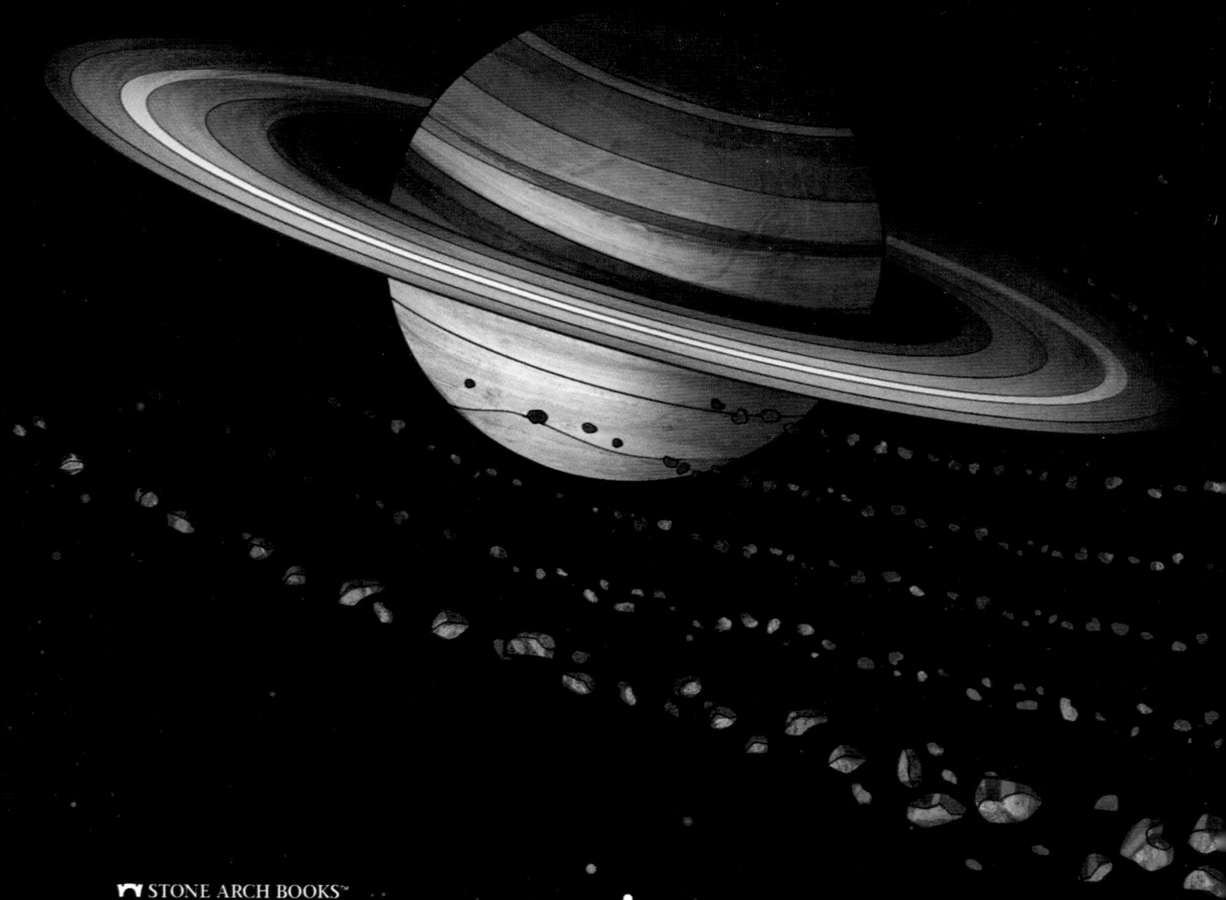

STONE ARCH BOOKS™

Published in 2013
A Capstone Imprint
1710 Roe Crest Drive
North Mankato, MN 56003
www.capstonepub.com

Originally published by DC Comics in the U.S. in single magazine form as Justice League Unlimited #7.

DC Comics
1700 Broadway, New York, NY 10019
A Warner Bros. Entertainment Company

Printed in China by Nordica.
0413/CA21300442
032013 007226NORDF13

Cataloging-in-Publication Data is available at the Library of Congress website:
ISBN: 978-1-4342-6043-7 (library binding)

Summary: The Justice League is assembled to help Orion and the New Gods stop Darkseid from unleashing his new weapon: the X-Cannon, which is powerful enough to destroy the Source Wall and give Darkseid access to the one thing he wants above all else: the Anti-Life Equation!

STONE ARCH BOOKS

Ashley C. Andersen Zantop *Publisher*
Michael Dahl *Editorial Director*
Sean Tulien & Donald Lemke *Editors*
Heather Kindseth *Creative Director*
Bob Lentz & Hilary Wacholz *Designers*
Kathy McColley *Production Specialist*

DC COMICS

Tom Palmer Jr. *Original U.S. Editor*

JUSTICE LEAGUE UNLIMITED

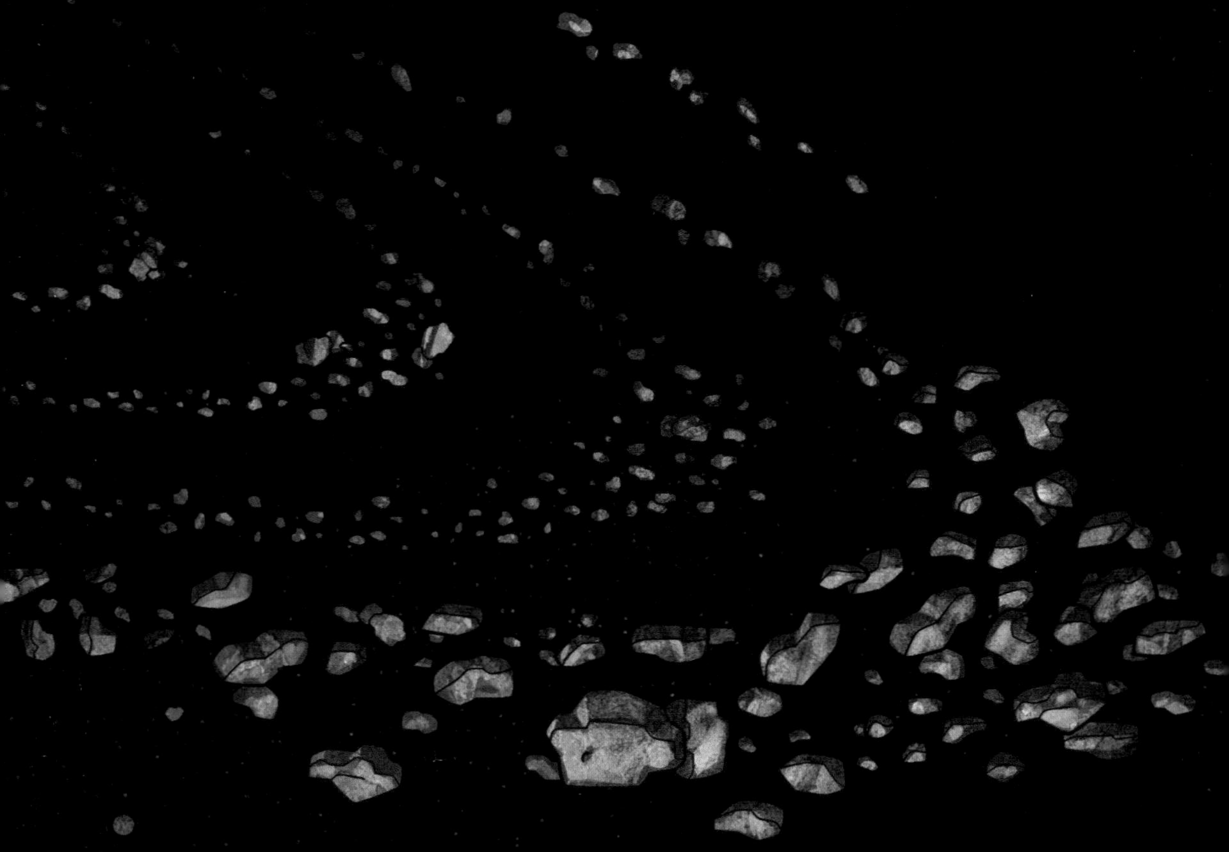

DARKSEID'S INFERNO!

Adam Beechen.. writer
Ethan Beavers..artist
Heroic Age ....colorist
Nick J. Napolitano ....letterer

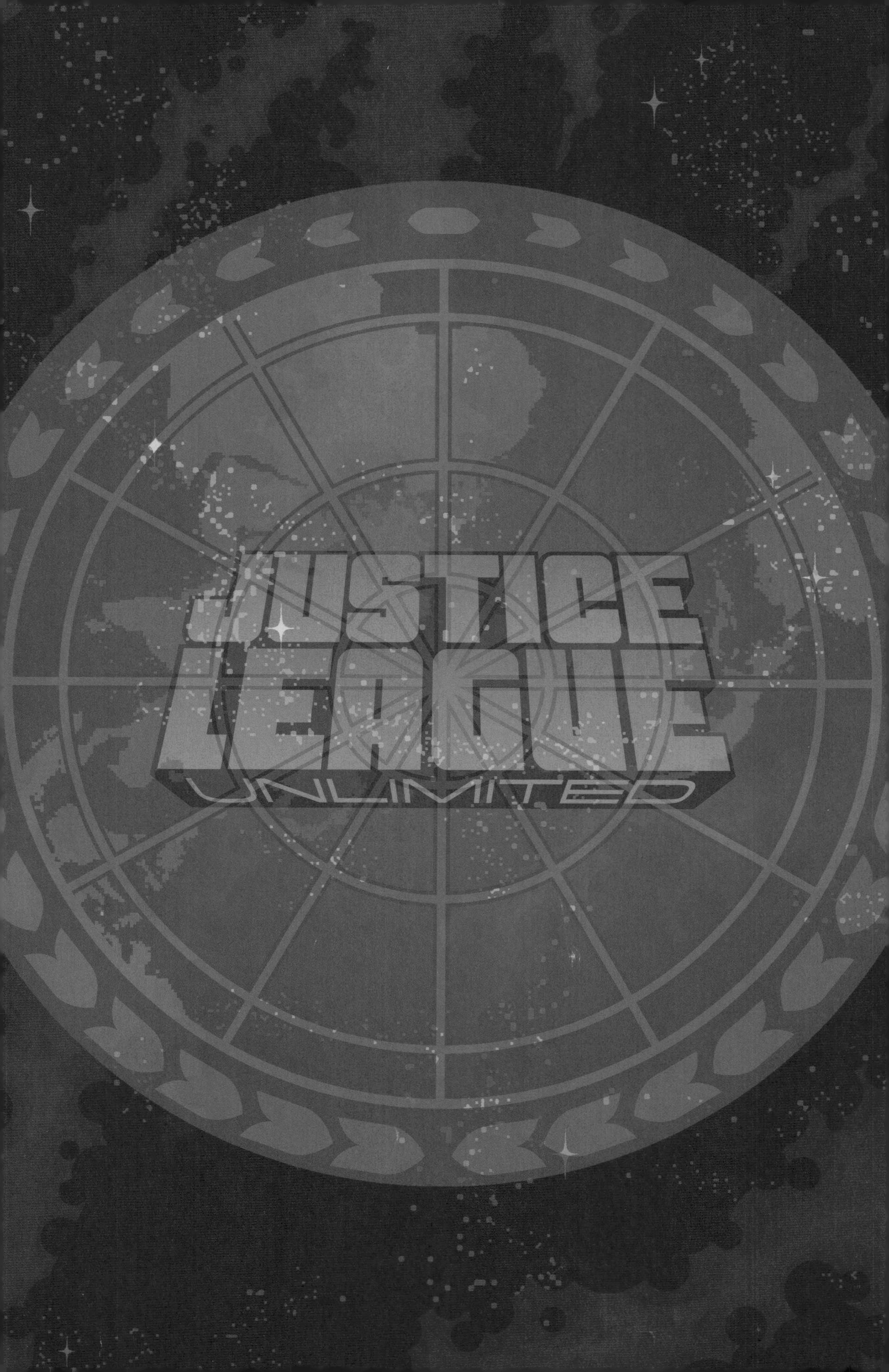
JUSTICE LEAGUE
UNLIMITED

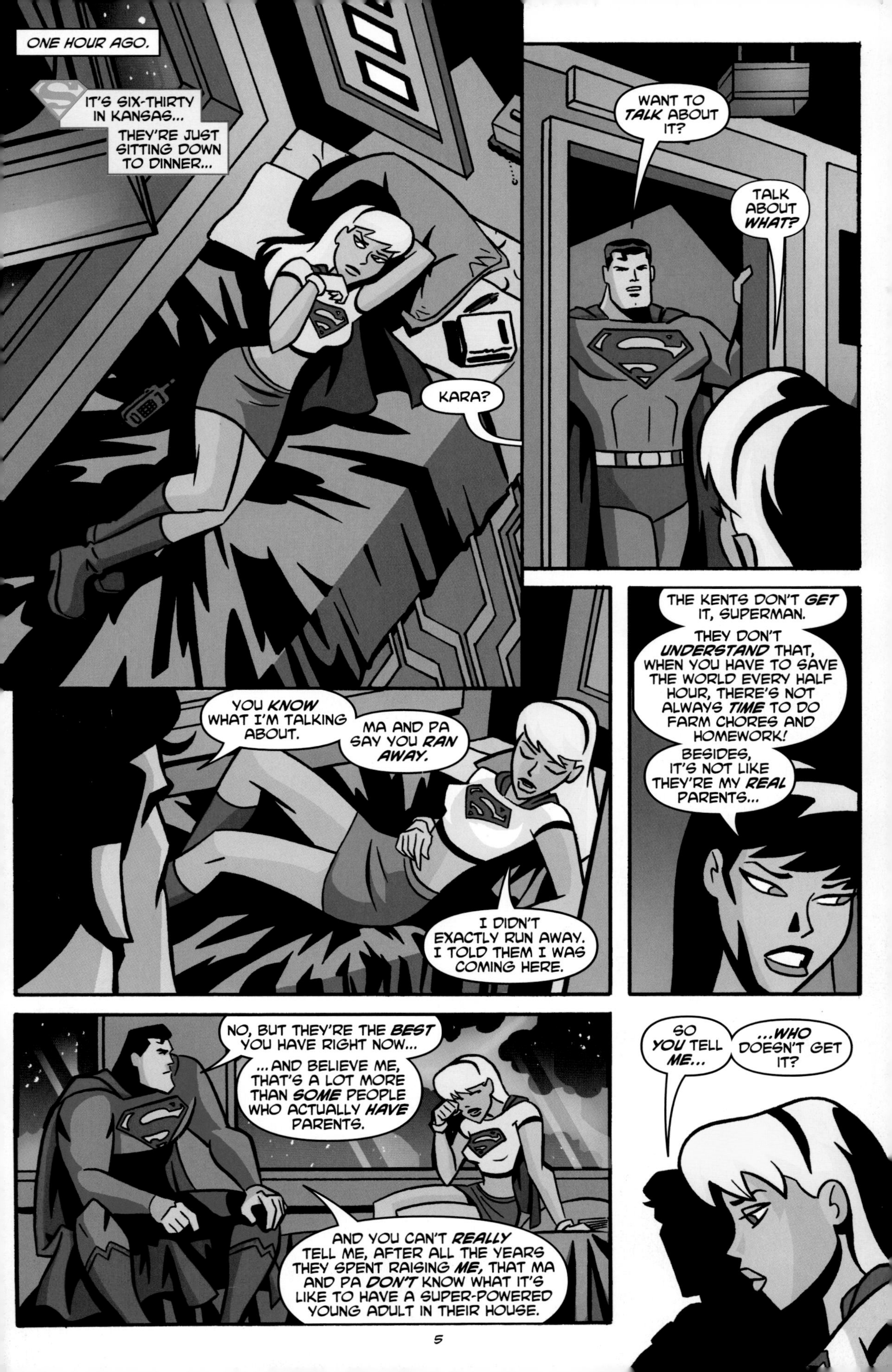

ONE HOUR AGO.
IT'S SIX-THIRTY IN KANSAS...
THEY'RE JUST SITTING DOWN TO DINNER...
KARA?
WANT TO TALK ABOUT IT?
TALK ABOUT WHAT?
YOU KNOW WHAT I'M TALKING ABOUT.
MA AND PA SAY YOU RAN AWAY.
I DIDN'T EXACTLY RUN AWAY. I TOLD THEM I WAS COMING HERE.
THE KENTS DON'T GET IT, SUPERMAN.
THEY DON'T UNDERSTAND THAT, WHEN YOU HAVE TO SAVE THE WORLD EVERY HALF HOUR, THERE'S NOT ALWAYS TIME TO DO FARM CHORES AND HOMEWORK!
BESIDES, IT'S NOT LIKE THEY'RE MY REAL PARENTS...
NO, BUT THEY'RE THE BEST YOU HAVE RIGHT NOW...
...AND BELIEVE ME, THAT'S A LOT MORE THAN SOME PEOPLE WHO ACTUALLY HAVE PARENTS.
AND YOU CAN'T REALLY TELL ME, AFTER ALL THE YEARS THEY SPENT RAISING ME, THAT MA AND PA DON'T KNOW WHAT IT'S LIKE TO HAVE A SUPER-POWERED YOUNG ADULT IN THEIR HOUSE.
SO YOU TELL ME...
...WHO DOESN'T GET IT?

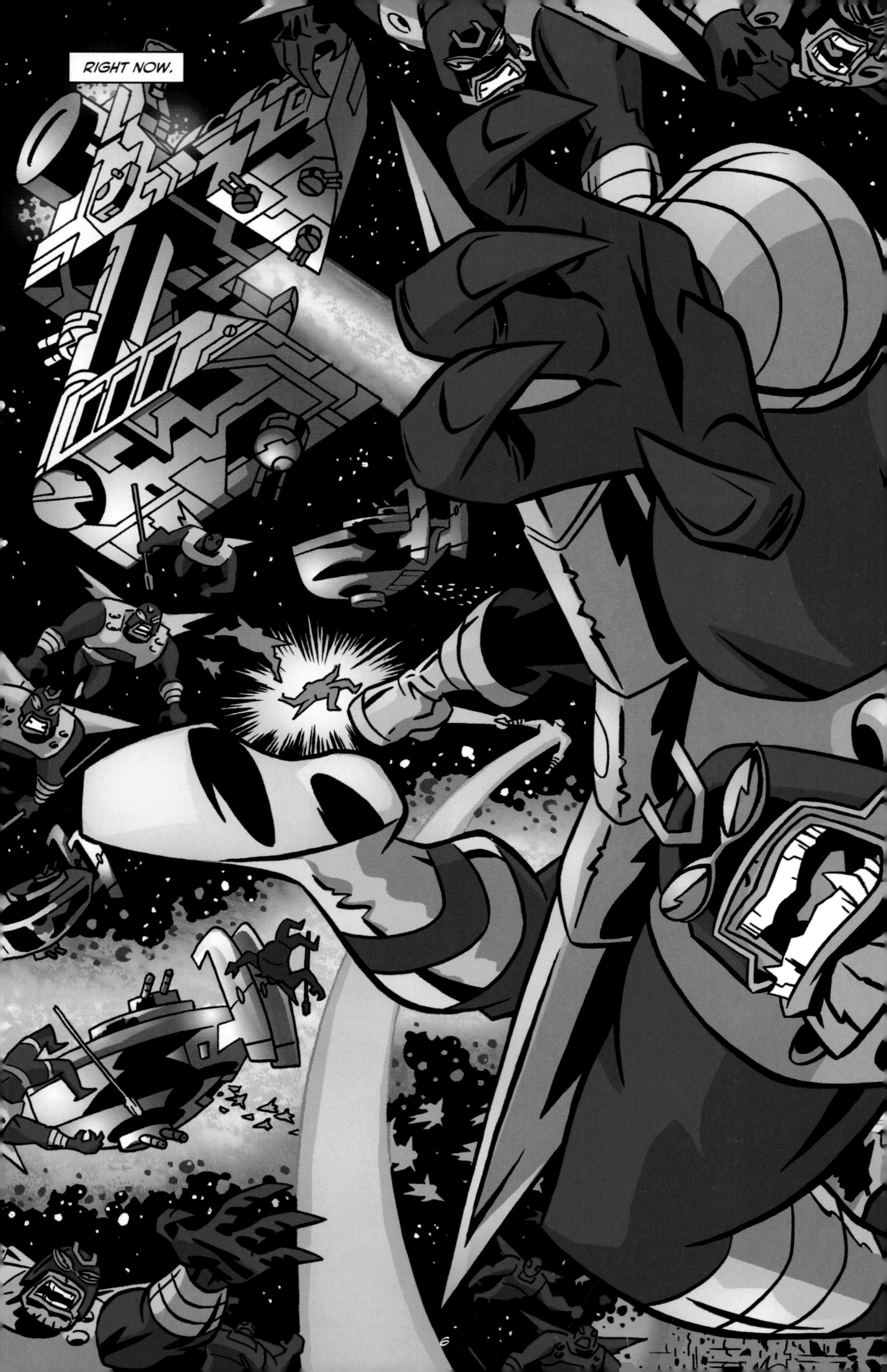
RIGHT NOW.

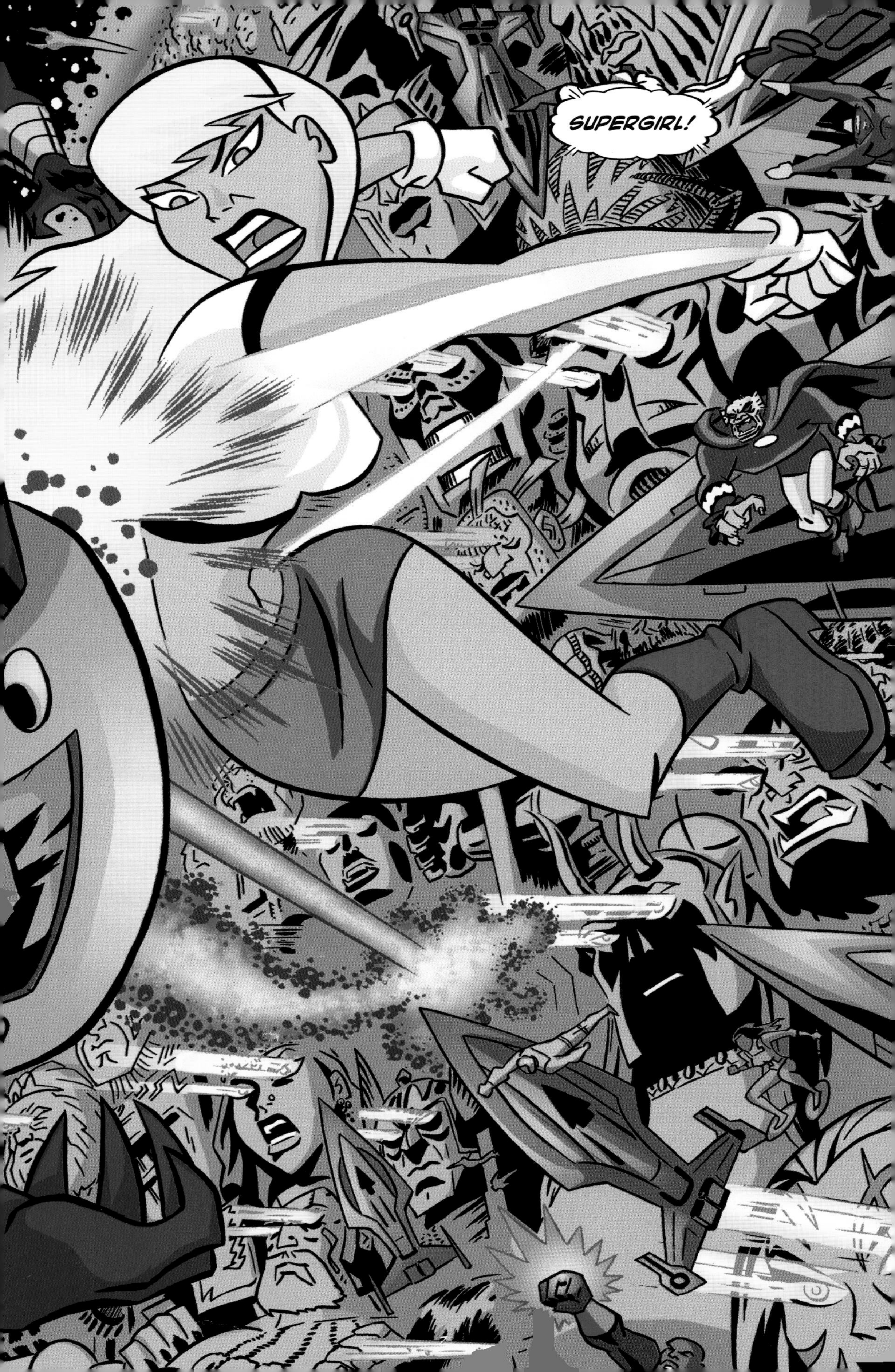
SUPERGIRL!

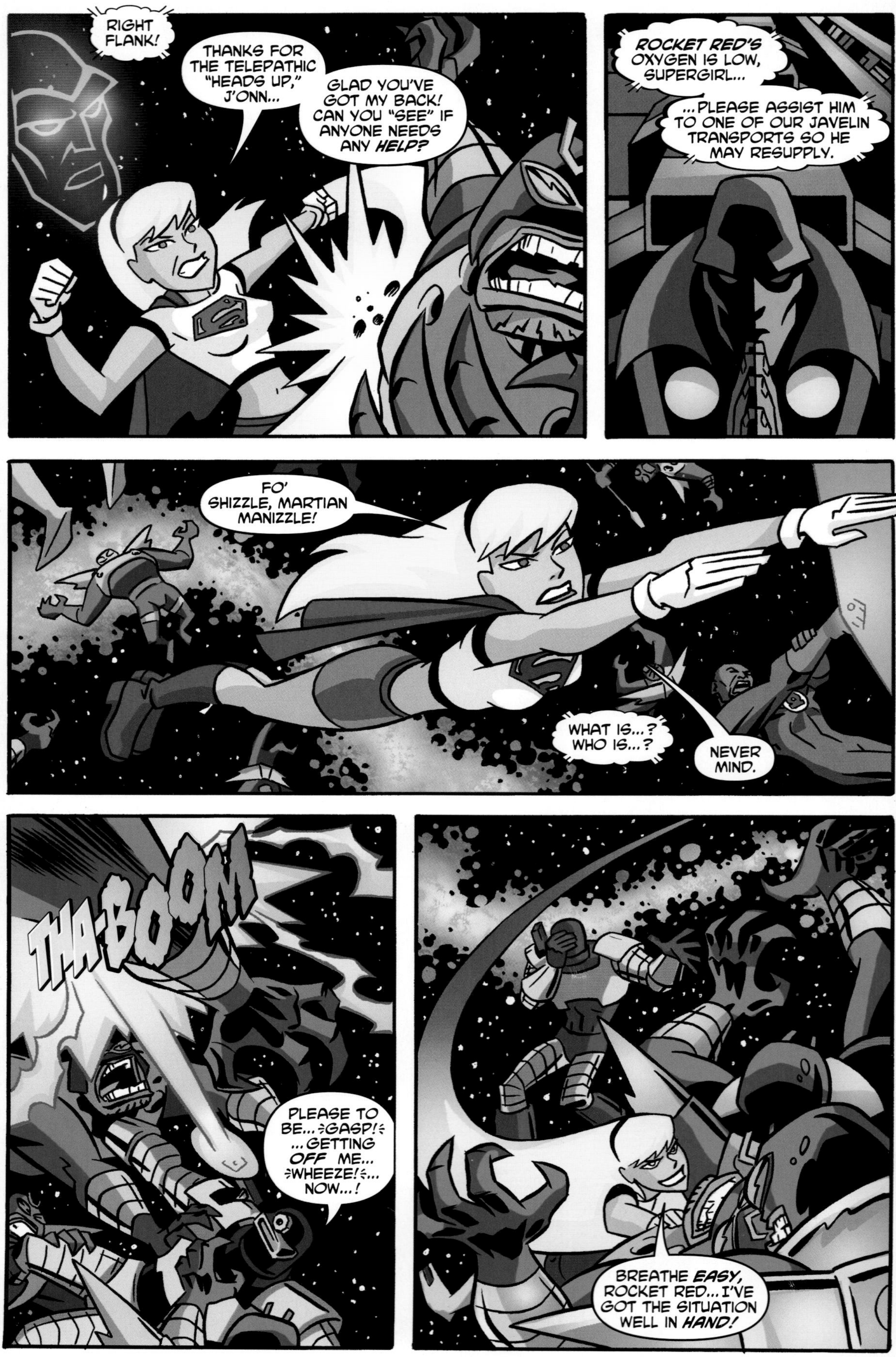
RIGHT FLANK!
THANKS FOR THE TELEPATHIC "HEADS UP," J'ONN...
GLAD YOU'VE GOT MY BACK! CAN YOU "SEE" IF ANYONE NEEDS ANY HELP?
ROCKET RED'S OXYGEN IS LOW, SUPERGIRL...
...PLEASE ASSIST HIM TO ONE OF OUR JAVELIN TRANSPORTS SO HE MAY RESUPPLY.
FO' SHIZZLE, MARTIAN MANIZZLE!
WHAT IS...? WHO IS...?
NEVER MIND.
THA-BOOM
PLEASE TO BE... GASP! ...GETTING OFF ME... WHEEZE!... NOW...!
BREATHE EASY, ROCKET RED... I'VE GOT THE SITUATION WELL IN HAND!

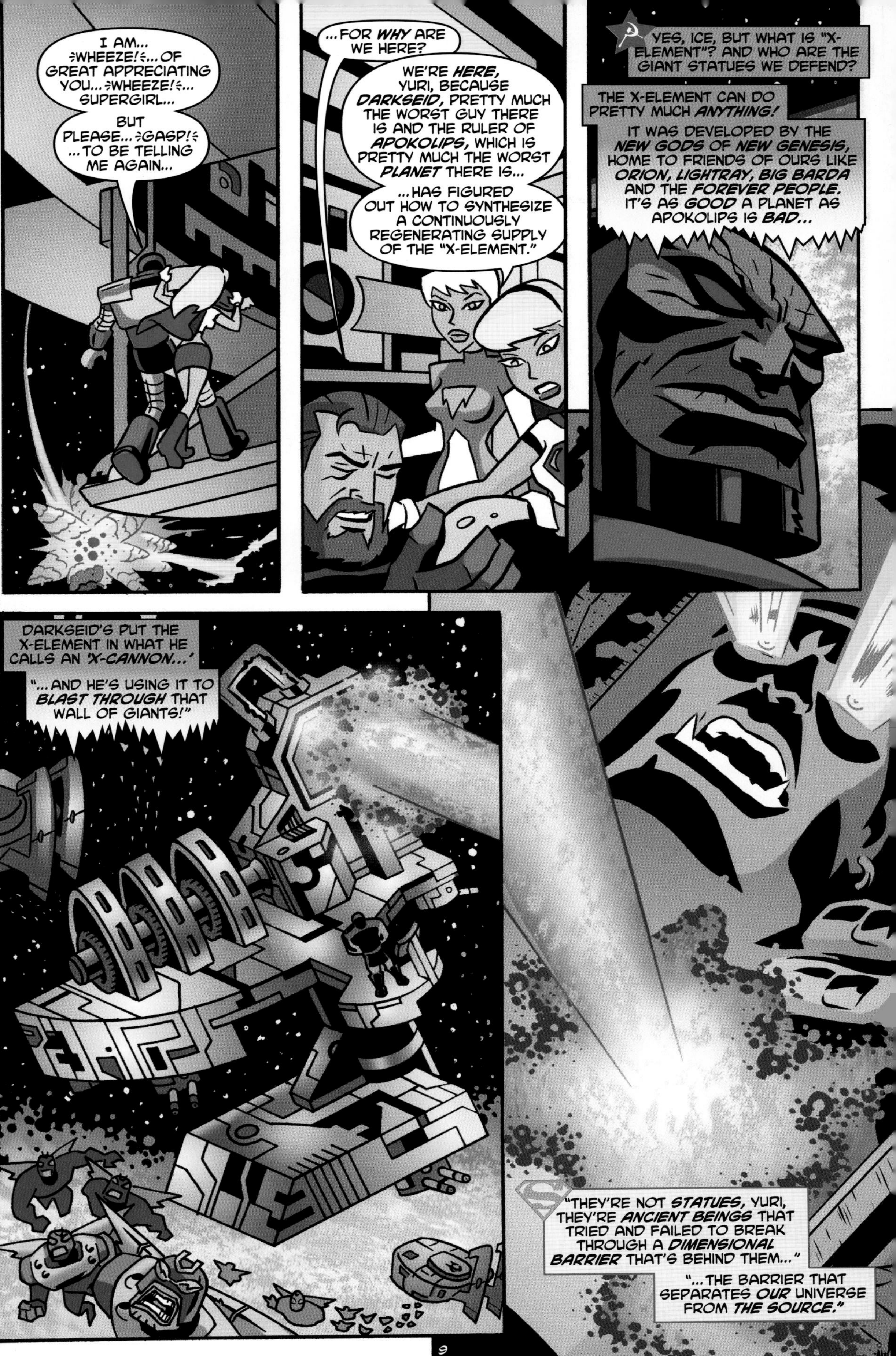
I AM... ⁑WHEEZE!⁑... OF GREAT APPRECIATING YOU... ⁑WHEEZE!⁑... SUPERGIRL...
BUT PLEASE... ⁑GASP!⁑ ...TO BE TELLING ME AGAIN...
...FOR WHY ARE WE HERE?
WE'RE HERE, YURI, BECAUSE DARKSEID, PRETTY MUCH THE WORST GUY THERE IS AND THE RULER OF APOKOLIPS, WHICH IS PRETTY MUCH THE WORST PLANET THERE IS...
...HAS FIGURED OUT HOW TO SYNTHESIZE A CONTINUOUSLY REGENERATING SUPPLY OF THE "X-ELEMENT."
YES, ICE, BUT WHAT IS "X-ELEMENT"? AND WHO ARE THE GIANT STATUES WE DEFEND?
THE X-ELEMENT CAN DO PRETTY MUCH ANYTHING!
IT WAS DEVELOPED BY THE NEW GODS OF NEW GENESIS, HOME TO FRIENDS OF OURS LIKE ORION, LIGHTRAY, BIG BARDA AND THE FOREVER PEOPLE. IT'S AS GOOD A PLANET AS APOKOLIPS IS BAD...
DARKSEID'S PUT THE X-ELEMENT IN WHAT HE CALLS AN 'X-CANNON...'
"...AND HE'S USING IT TO BLAST THROUGH THAT WALL OF GIANTS!"
"THEY'RE NOT STATUES, YURI, THEY'RE ANCIENT BEINGS THAT TRIED AND FAILED TO BREAK THROUGH A DIMENSIONAL BARRIER THAT'S BEHIND THEM..."
"...THE BARRIER THAT SEPARATES OUR UNIVERSE FROM THE SOURCE."

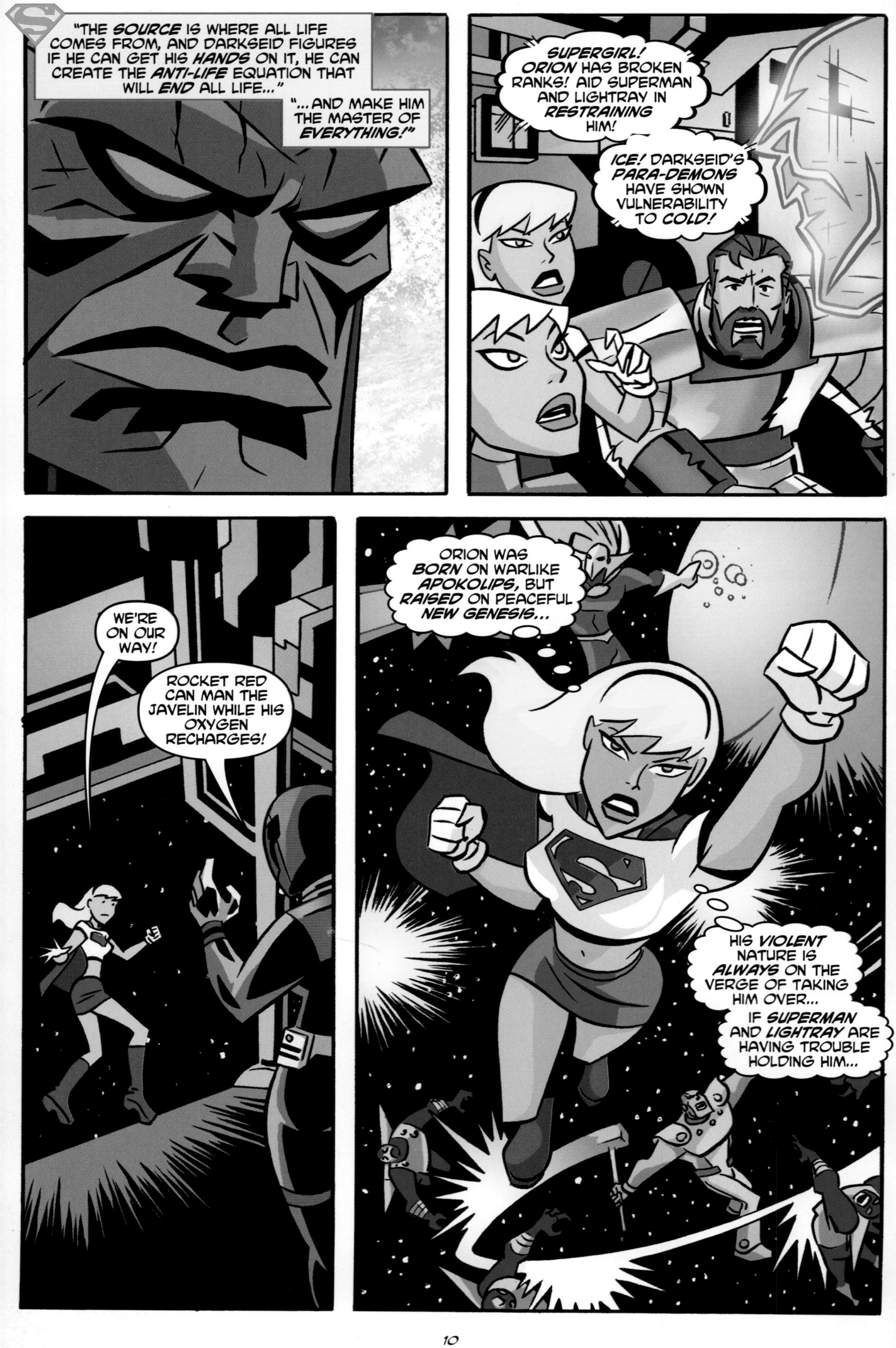
"THE SOURCE IS WHERE ALL LIFE COMES FROM, AND DARKSEID FIGURES IF HE CAN GET HIS HANDS ON IT, HE CAN CREATE THE ANTI-LIFE EQUATION THAT WILL END ALL LIFE..."
"...AND MAKE HIM THE MASTER OF EVERYTHING!"
SUPERGIRL! ORION HAS BROKEN RANKS! AID SUPERMAN AND LIGHTRAY IN RESTRAINING HIM!
ICE! DARKSEID'S PARA-DEMONS HAVE SHOWN VULNERABILITY TO COLD!
WE'RE ON OUR WAY!
ROCKET RED CAN MAN THE JAVELIN WHILE HIS OXYGEN RECHARGES!
ORION WAS BORN ON WARLIKE APOKOLIPS, BUT RAISED ON PEACEFUL NEW GENESIS...
HIS VIOLENT NATURE IS ALWAYS ON THE VERGE OF TAKING HIM OVER...
IF SUPERMAN AND LIGHTRAY ARE HAVING TROUBLE HOLDING HIM...

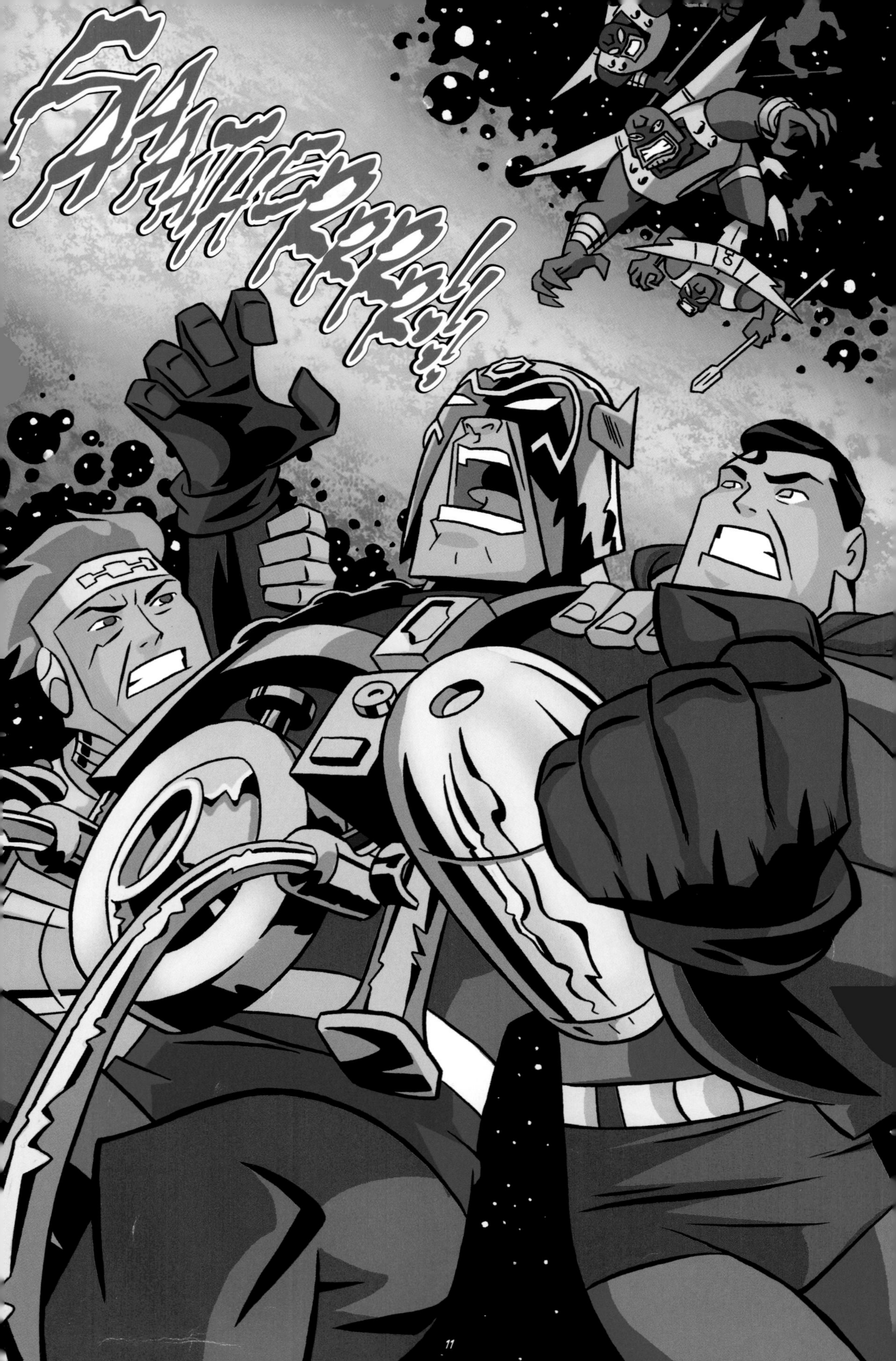
SHATTERRRR!!

WHY, *FATHER?* WHY MUST YOU DEVOTE YOURSELF TO *DESTRUCTION* AND *TYRANNY?*

IT IS NOT FOR *YOU* TO QUESTION MY ACTIONS, MY SON...

DARKSEID DOES AS HE *WILL.* AS HE *MUST.*

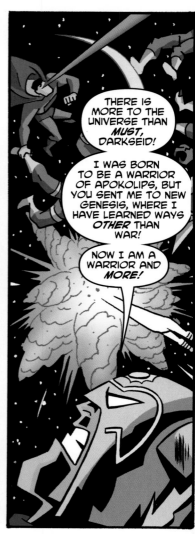

THERE IS MORE TO THE UNIVERSE THAN *MUST,* DARKSEID!

I WAS BORN TO BE A WARRIOR OF APOKOLIPS, BUT YOU SENT ME TO NEW GENESIS, WHERE I HAVE LEARNED WAYS *OTHER* THAN WAR!

NOW I AM A WARRIOR AND *MORE!*

BE WHAT YOU WISH, ORION. DARKSEID IS *DARKSEID.*

I WILL DO WHAT I WILL DO.

THEN LET *THIS* BE THE DAY THE PROPHECIES BECOME *TRUE!*

LET *THIS* BE THE DAY ORION *ENDS* HIS FATHER'S REIGN OF TERROR!

ORION! *WAIT,* MY FRIEND!

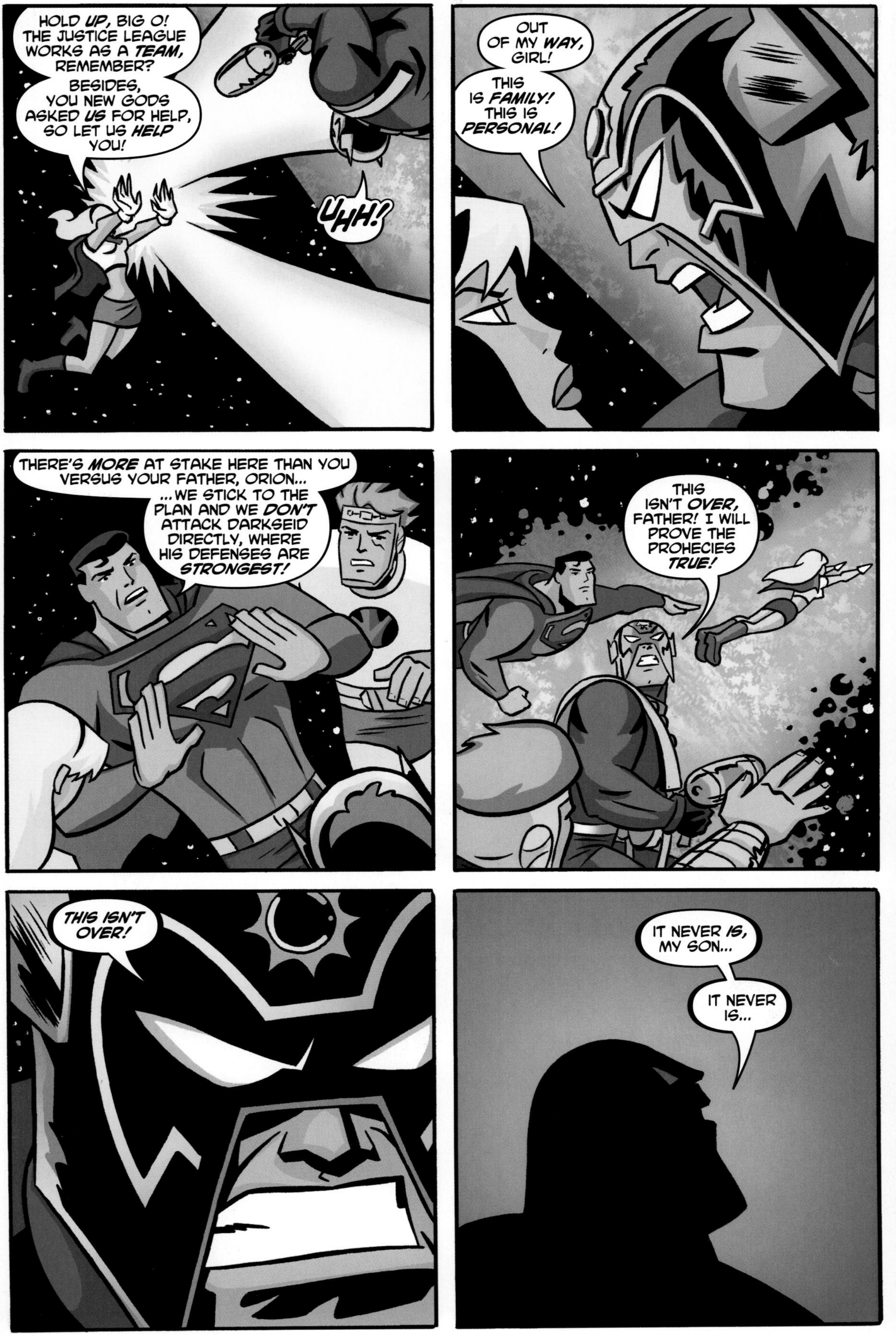
HOLD UP, BIG O! THE JUSTICE LEAGUE WORKS AS A TEAM, REMEMBER?
BESIDES, YOU NEW GODS ASKED US FOR HELP, SO LET US HELP YOU!
UHH!
OUT OF MY WAY, GIRL!
THIS IS FAMILY! THIS IS PERSONAL!
THERE'S MORE AT STAKE HERE THAN YOU VERSUS YOUR FATHER, ORION...
...WE STICK TO THE PLAN AND WE DON'T ATTACK DARKSEID DIRECTLY, WHERE HIS DEFENSES ARE STRONGEST!
THIS ISN'T OVER, FATHER! I WILL PROVE THE PROHECIES TRUE!
THIS ISN'T OVER!
IT NEVER IS, MY SON...
IT NEVER IS...

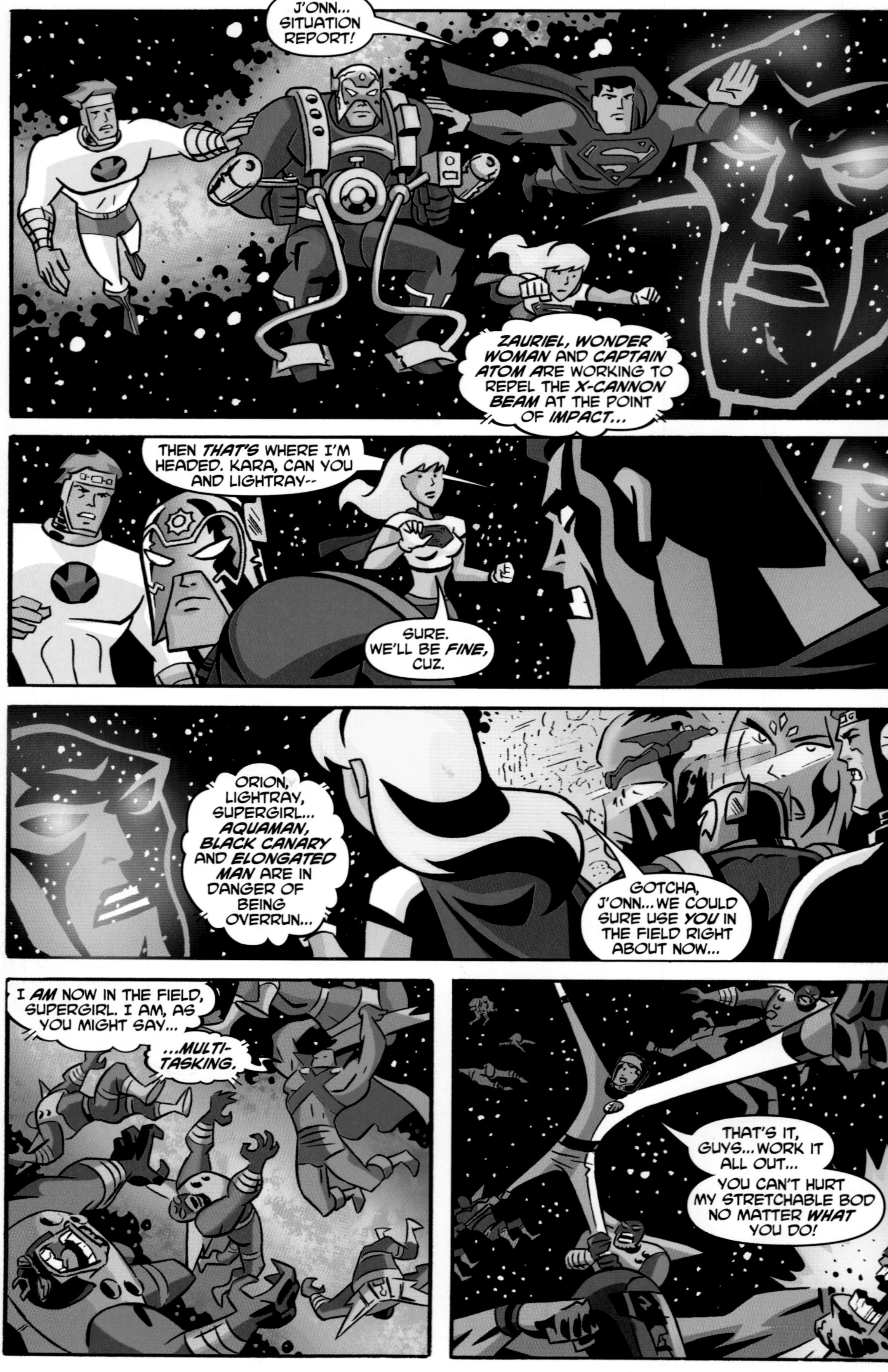
J'ONN... SITUATION REPORT!
ZAURIEL, WONDER WOMAN AND CAPTAIN ATOM ARE WORKING TO REPEL THE X-CANNON BEAM AT THE POINT OF IMPACT...
THEN THAT'S WHERE I'M HEADED. KARA, CAN YOU AND LIGHTRAY--
SURE. WE'LL BE FINE, CUZ.
ORION, LIGHTRAY, SUPERGIRL... AQUAMAN, BLACK CANARY AND ELONGATED MAN ARE IN DANGER OF BEING OVERRUN...
GOTCHA, J'ONN... WE COULD SURE USE YOU IN THE FIELD RIGHT ABOUT NOW...
I AM NOW IN THE FIELD, SUPERGIRL. I AM, AS YOU MIGHT SAY...
...MULTI-TASKING.
THAT'S IT, GUYS... WORK IT ALL OUT...
YOU CAN'T HURT MY STRETCHABLE BOD NO MATTER WHAT YOU DO!

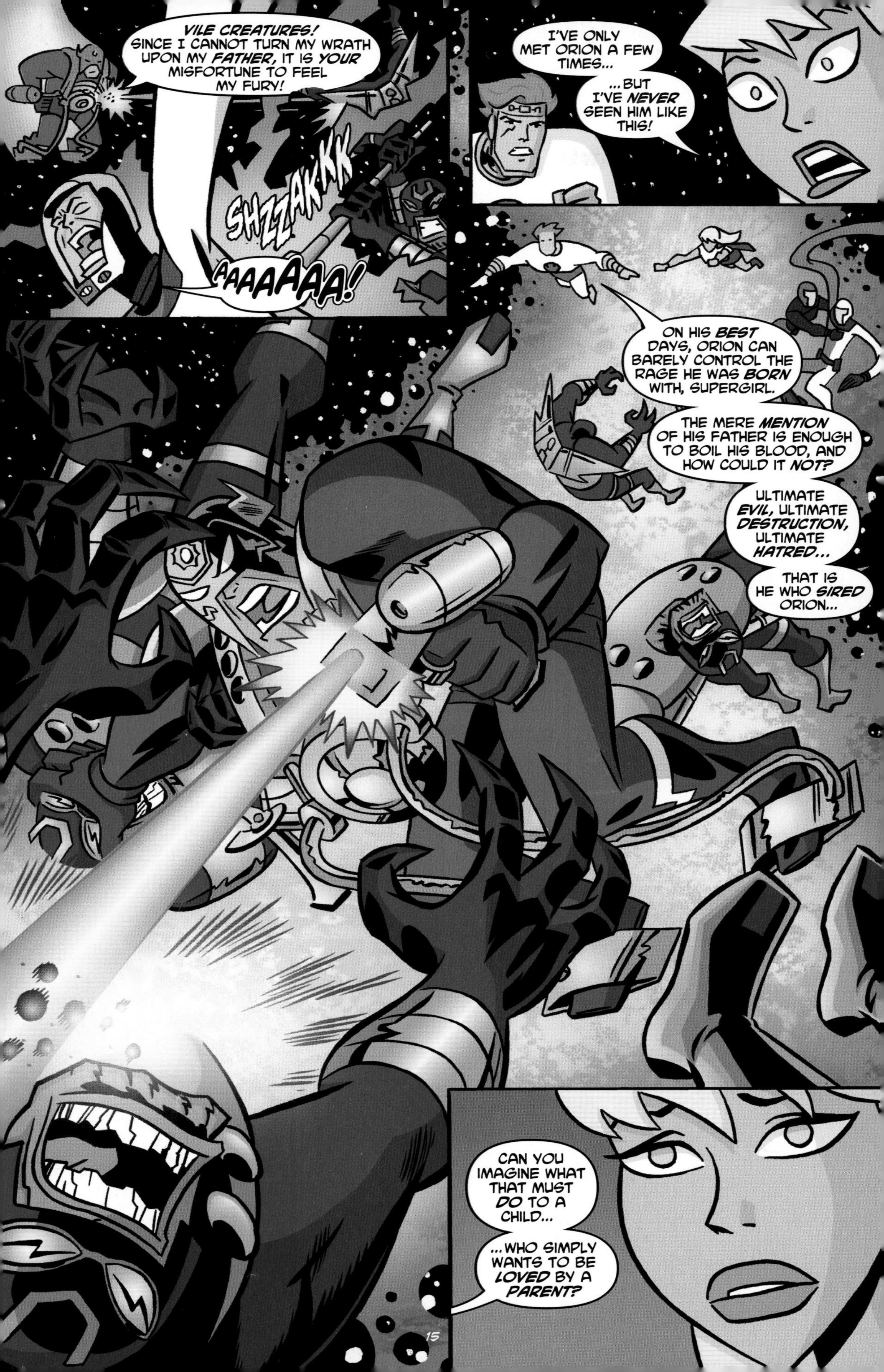
VILE CREATURES! SINCE I CANNOT TURN MY WRATH UPON MY FATHER, IT IS YOUR MISFORTUNE TO FEEL MY FURY!
SHZZAKKK
AAAAAAA!
I'VE ONLY MET ORION A FEW TIMES...
...BUT I'VE NEVER SEEN HIM LIKE THIS!
ON HIS BEST DAYS, ORION CAN BARELY CONTROL THE RAGE HE WAS BORN WITH, SUPERGIRL.
THE MERE MENTION OF HIS FATHER IS ENOUGH TO BOIL HIS BLOOD, AND HOW COULD IT NOT?
ULTIMATE EVIL, ULTIMATE DESTRUCTION, ULTIMATE HATRED...
THAT IS HE WHO SIRED ORION...
CAN YOU IMAGINE WHAT THAT MUST DO TO A CHILD...
...WHO SIMPLY WANTS TO BE LOVED BY A PARENT?

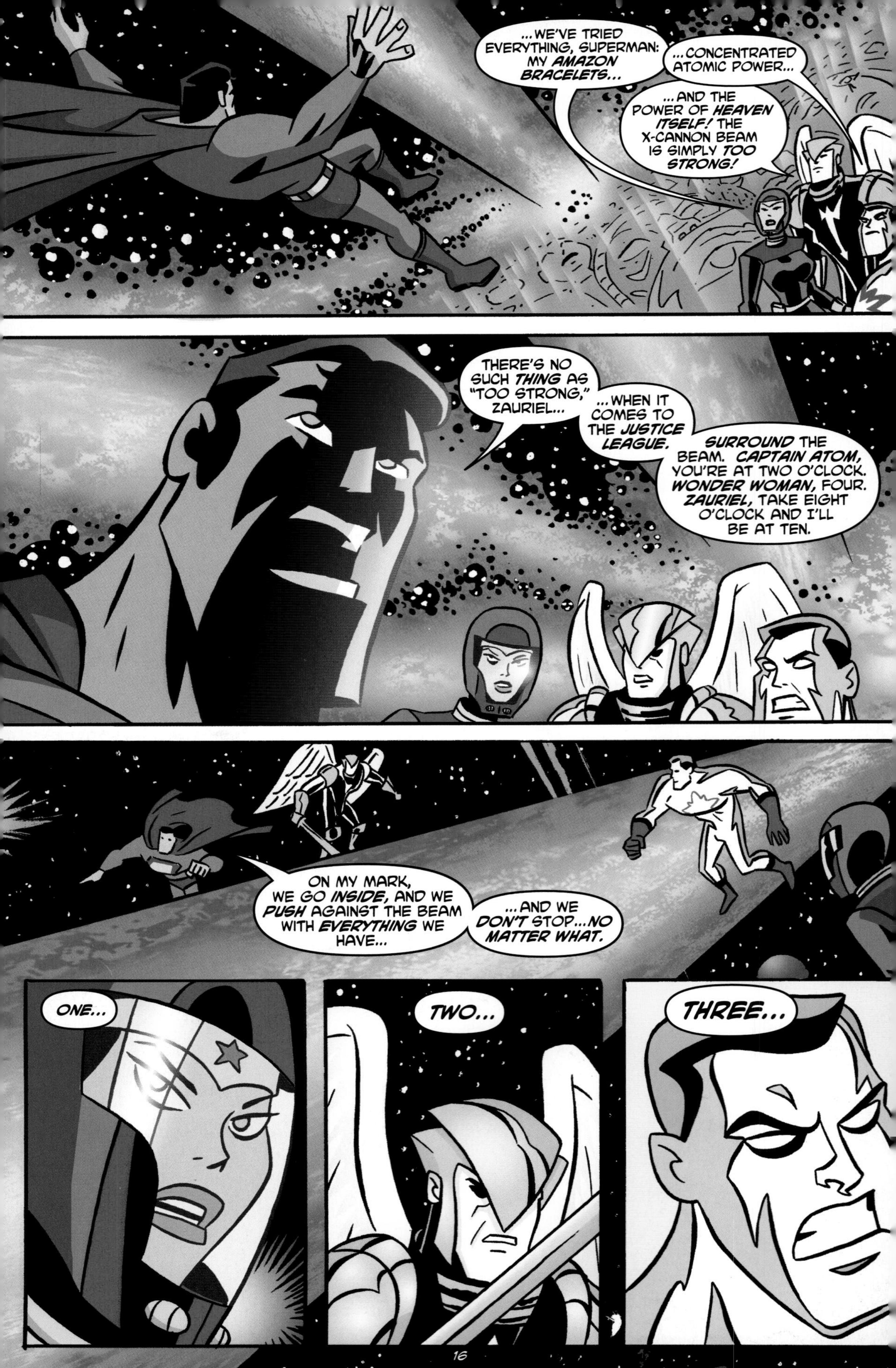
...WE'VE TRIED EVERYTHING, SUPERMAN: MY AMAZON BRACELETS...
...CONCENTRATED ATOMIC POWER...
...AND THE POWER OF HEAVEN ITSELF! THE X-CANNON BEAM IS SIMPLY TOO STRONG!
THERE'S NO SUCH THING AS "TOO STRONG," ZAURIEL...
...WHEN IT COMES TO THE JUSTICE LEAGUE.
SURROUND THE BEAM. CAPTAIN ATOM, YOU'RE AT TWO O'CLOCK. WONDER WOMAN, FOUR. ZAURIEL, TAKE EIGHT O'CLOCK AND I'LL BE AT TEN.
ON MY MARK, WE GO INSIDE, AND WE PUSH AGAINST THE BEAM WITH EVERYTHING WE HAVE...
...AND WE DON'T STOP...NO MATTER WHAT.
ONE...
TWO...
THREE...

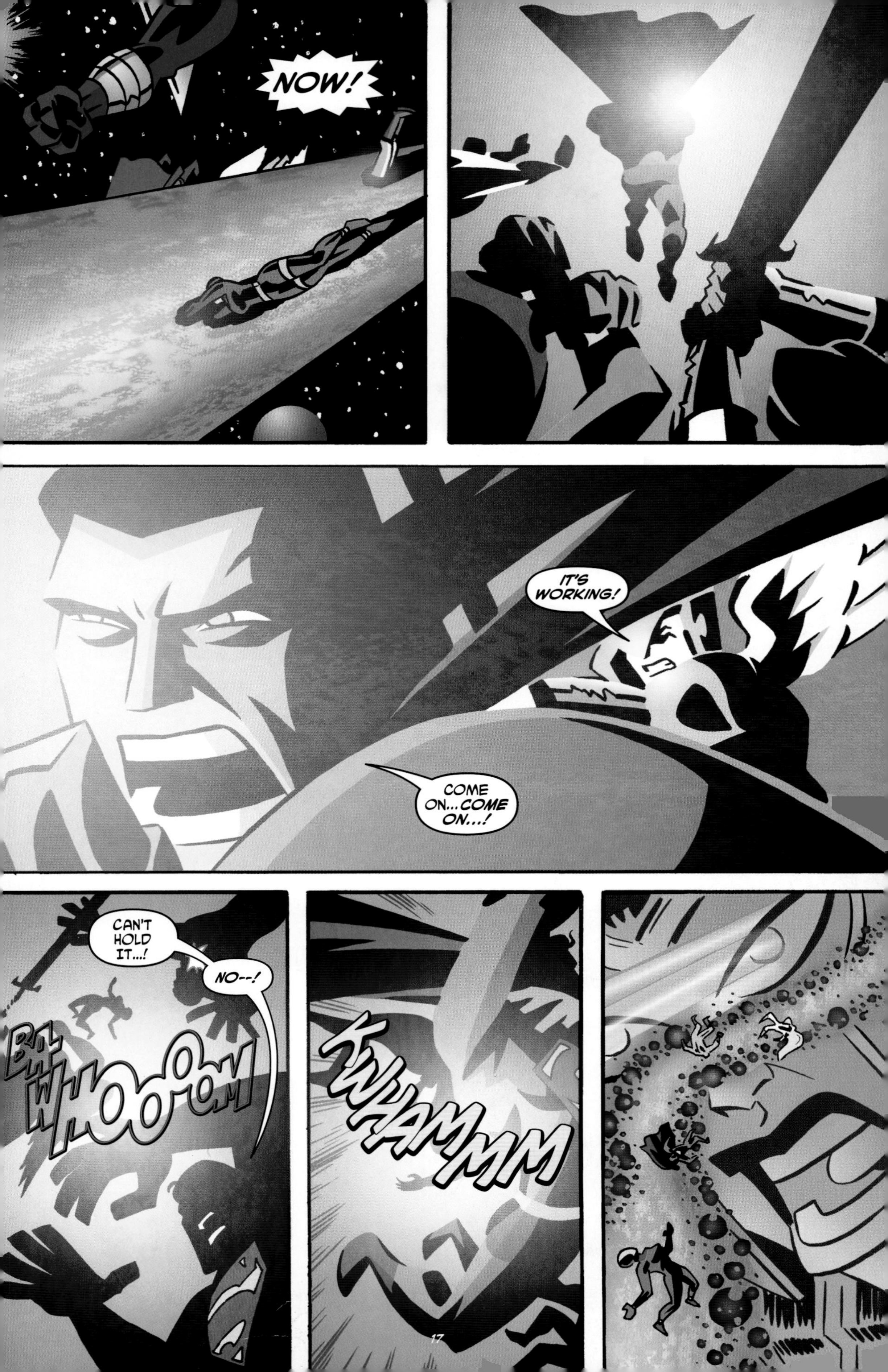
NOW!
IT'S WORKING!
COME ON...COME ON...!
CAN'T HOLD IT...!
NO--!
BA-WHOOOOOM
KWHAMMMM

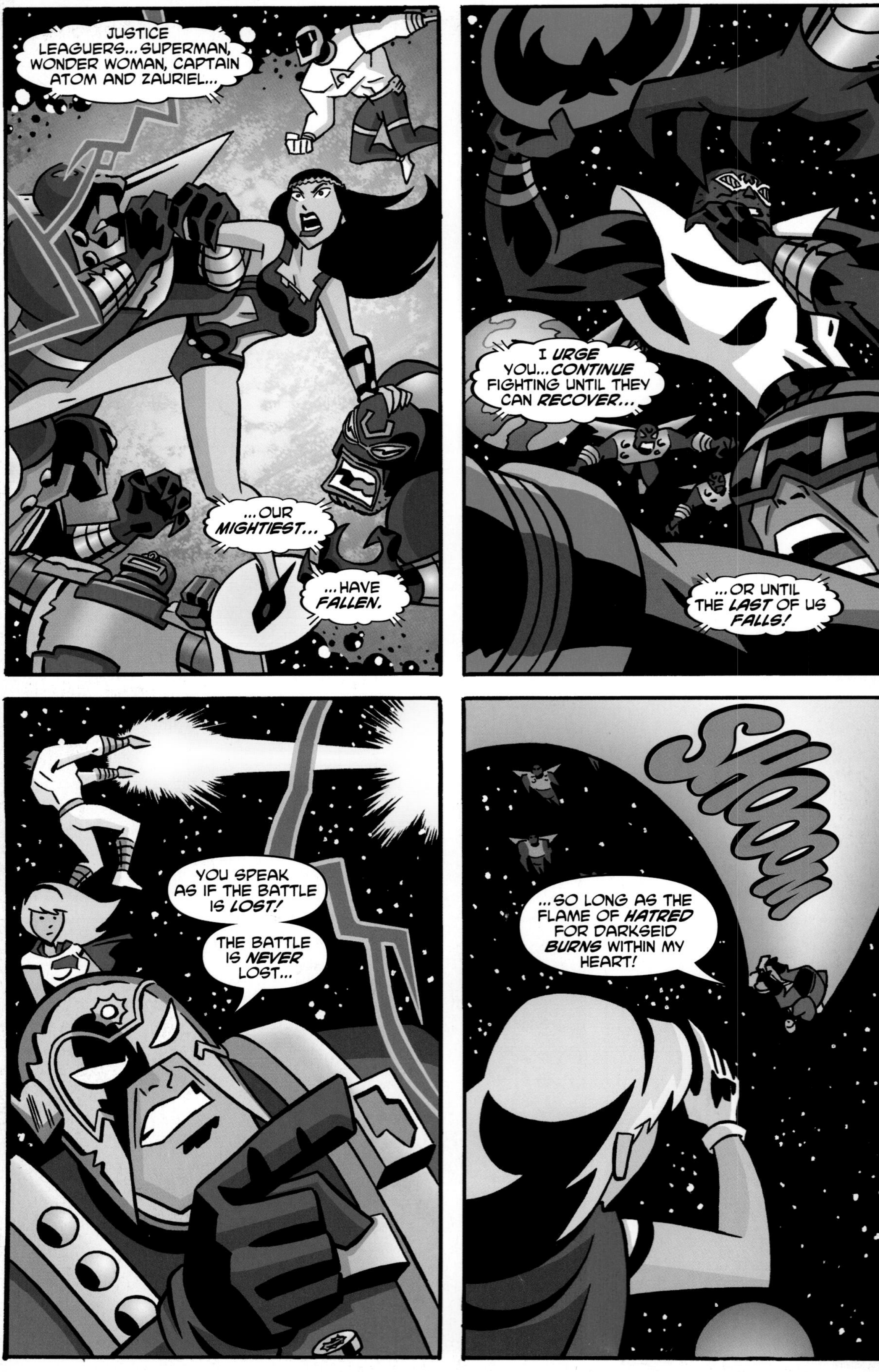
JUSTICE LEAGUERS... SUPERMAN, WONDER WOMAN, CAPTAIN ATOM AND ZAURIEL...
...OUR MIGHTIEST...
...HAVE FALLEN.
I URGE YOU...CONTINUE FIGHTING UNTIL THEY CAN RECOVER...
...OR UNTIL THE LAST OF US FALLS!
YOU SPEAK AS IF THE BATTLE IS LOST!
THE BATTLE IS NEVER LOST...
SHOOM
...SO LONG AS THE FLAME OF HATRED FOR DARKSEID BURNS WITHIN MY HEART!

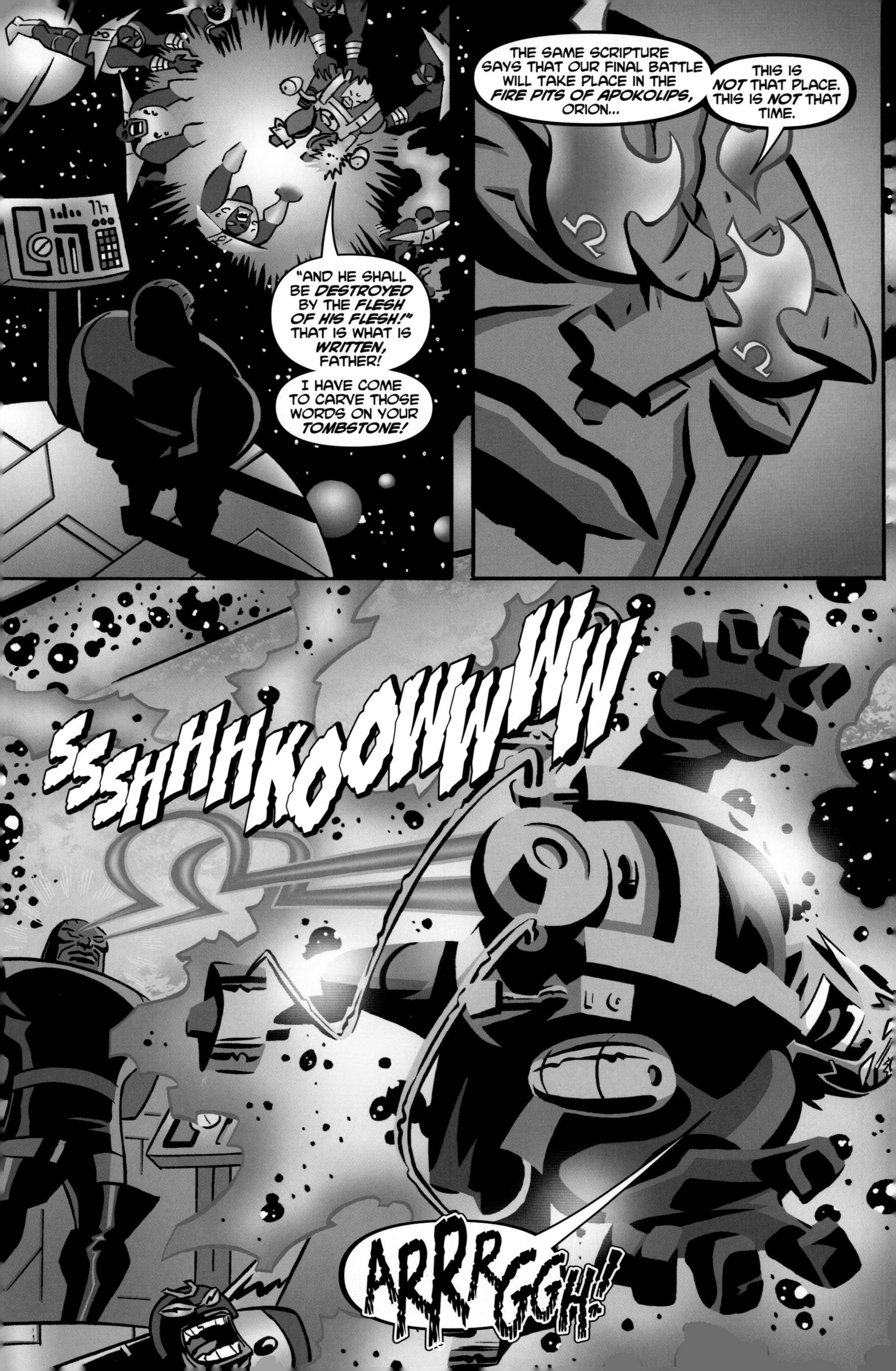
"AND HE SHALL BE DESTROYED BY THE FLESH OF HIS FLESH!" THAT IS WHAT IS WRITTEN, FATHER!
I HAVE COME TO CARVE THOSE WORDS ON YOUR TOMBSTONE!
THE SAME SCRIPTURE SAYS THAT OUR FINAL BATTLE WILL TAKE PLACE IN THE FIRE PITS OF APOKOLIPS, ORION...
THIS IS NOT THAT PLACE. THIS IS NOT THAT TIME.
SSSHHHKOOOWWWWW
ARRRGGH!

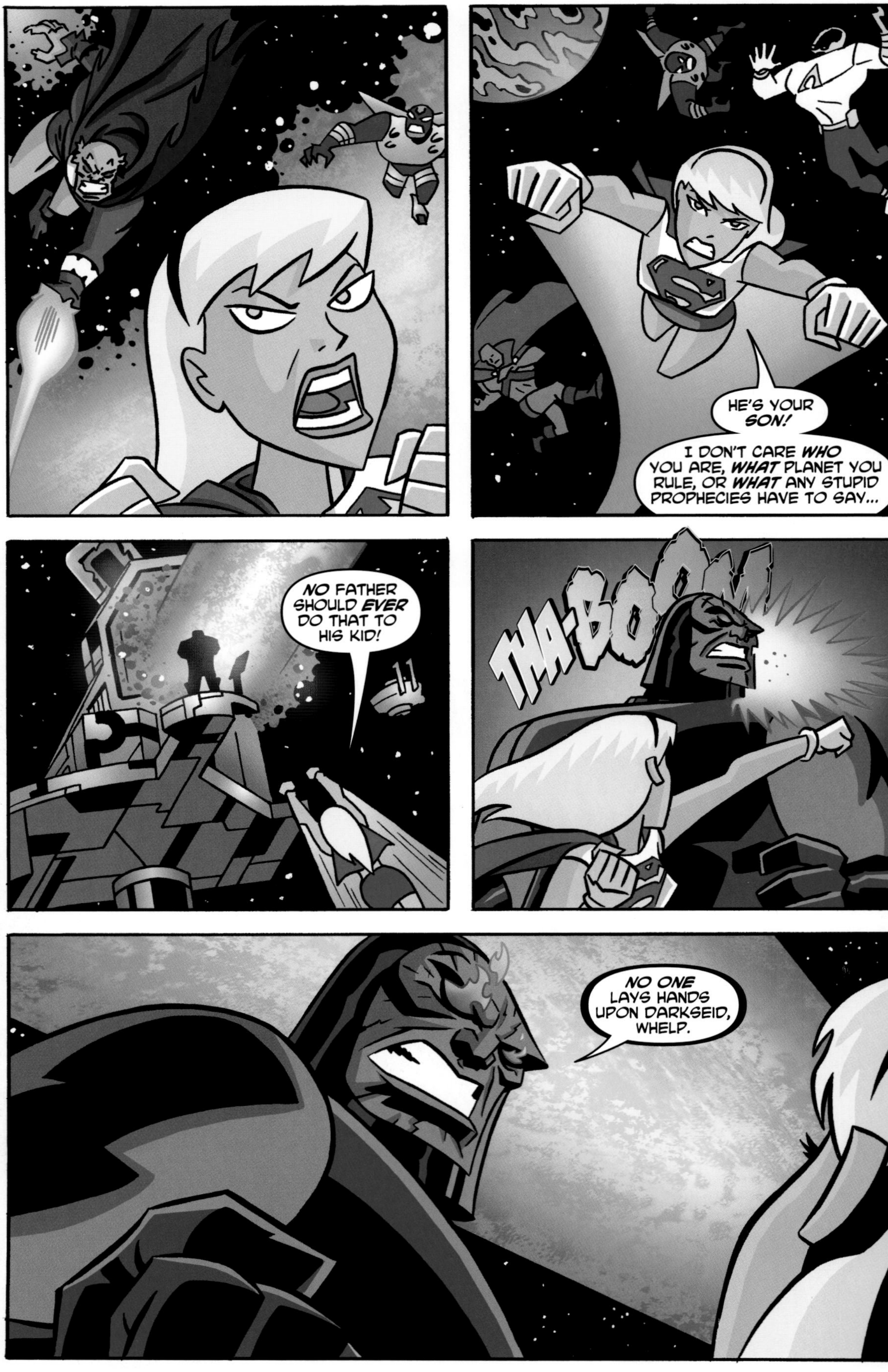
HE'S YOUR SON!
I DON'T CARE WHO YOU ARE, WHAT PLANET YOU RULE, OR WHAT ANY STUPID PROPHECIES HAVE TO SAY...
NO FATHER SHOULD EVER DO THAT TO HIS KID!
THA-BOOM
NO ONE LAYS HANDS UPON DARKSEID, WHELP.

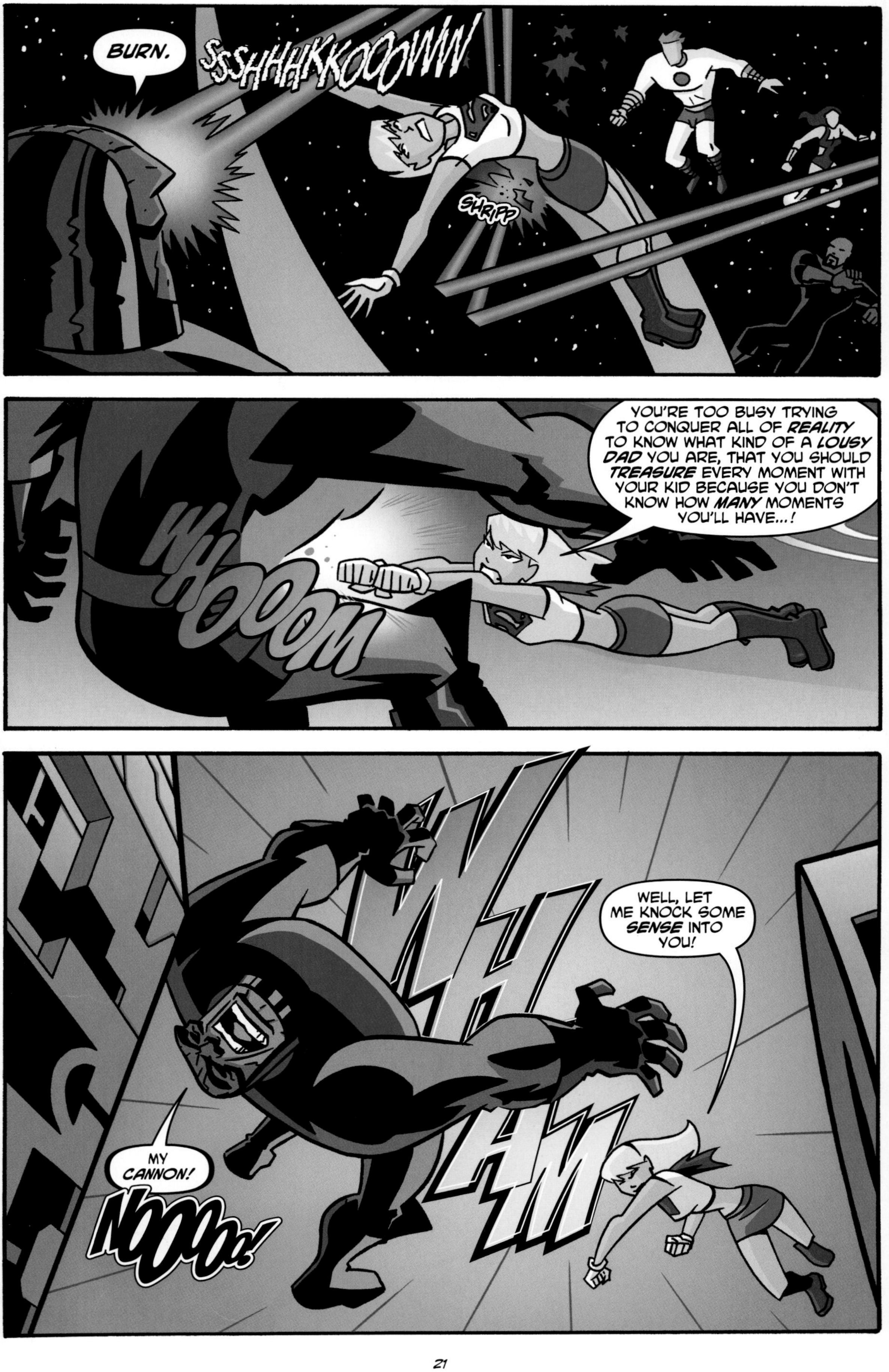
BURN.
SSHHHKKOOOWW
SHRIPP
YOU'RE TOO BUSY TRYING TO CONQUER ALL OF REALITY TO KNOW WHAT KIND OF A LOUSY DAD YOU ARE, THAT YOU SHOULD TREASURE EVERY MOMENT WITH YOUR KID BECAUSE YOU DON'T KNOW HOW MANY MOMENTS YOU'LL HAVE...!
WHOOOM
WELL, LET ME KNOCK SOME SENSE INTO YOU!
WHAM
MY CANNON!
NOOOoo!

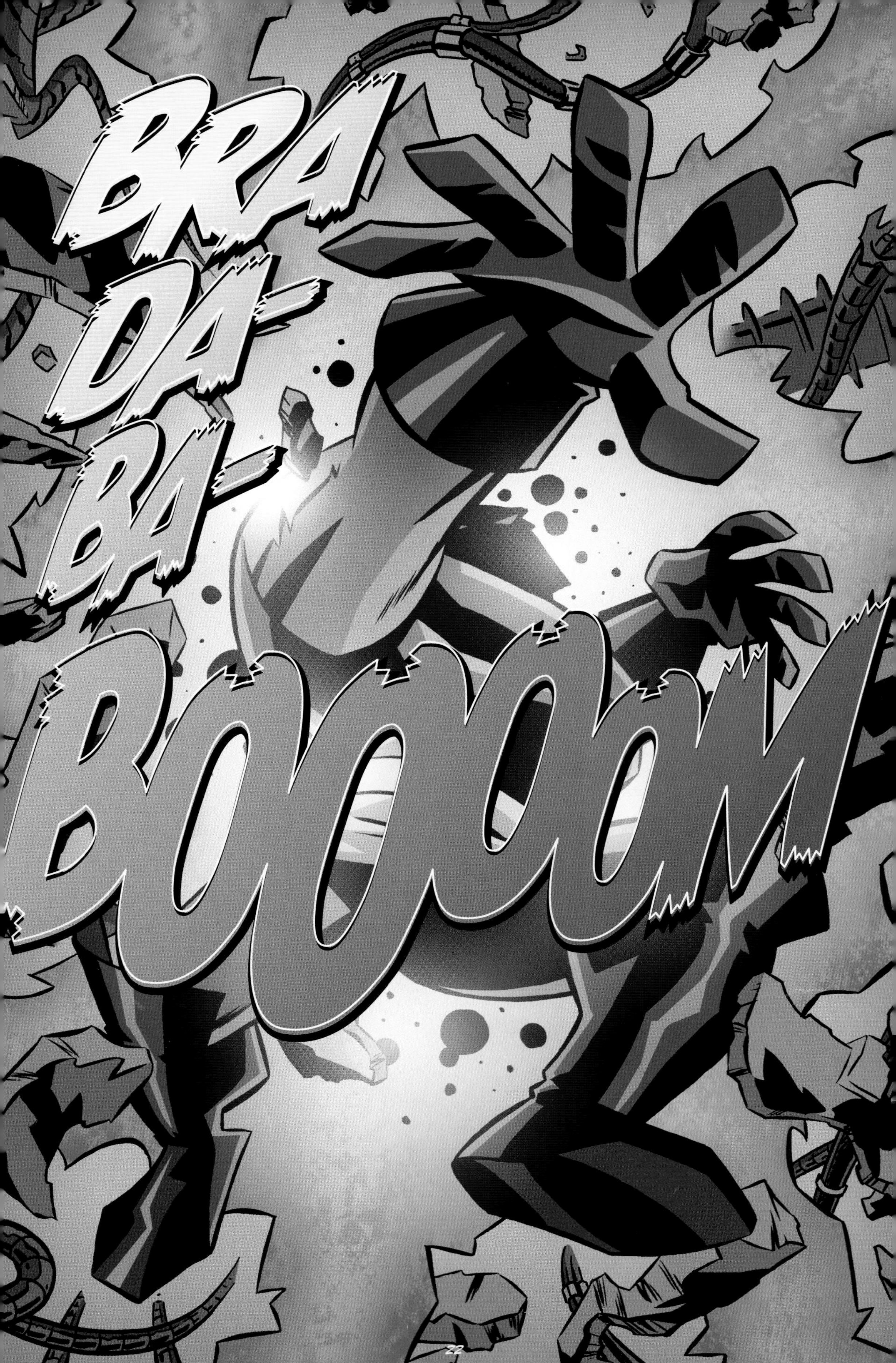
BRA-
DA-
BA-
BOOOOM

THE *X-ELEMENT*... THE *CANNON*... GONE...

BUT *DARKSEID* REMAINS. MY *DESTINY* REMAINS...

...NOTHING OF *IMPORTANCE* HAS CHANGED.

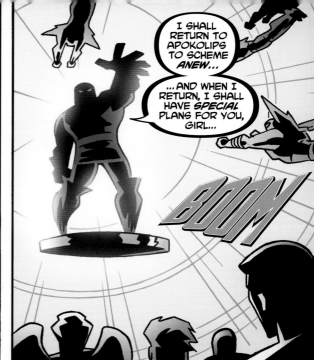

I SHALL RETURN TO APOKOLIPS TO SCHEME *ANEW*...

...AND WHEN I RETURN, I SHALL HAVE *SPECIAL* PLANS FOR YOU, *GIRL*...

BOOM

THE MOST POWERFUL MAN IN THE UNIVERSE, AND YOU TOOK HIS PLAN OUT WITH *ONE PUNCH!*

WOW, SUPERGIRL... REMIND ME NEVER TO MAKE *YOU* ANGRY!

YOUR BRAVERY WOULD MAKE YOU WORTHY OF A *HALLOWED PLACE* ON *NEW GENESIS*, SUPERGIRL.

THANKS, BIG BARDA...

I GUESS THAT BIG FREAKAZOID JUST GOT ME *MAD*, IS ALL...

THEN PERHAPS YOU KNOW A *FRACTION* OF WHAT IT IS TO BE *ORION*...

...AN *ORPHAN* WHOSE FATHER STILL LIVES.

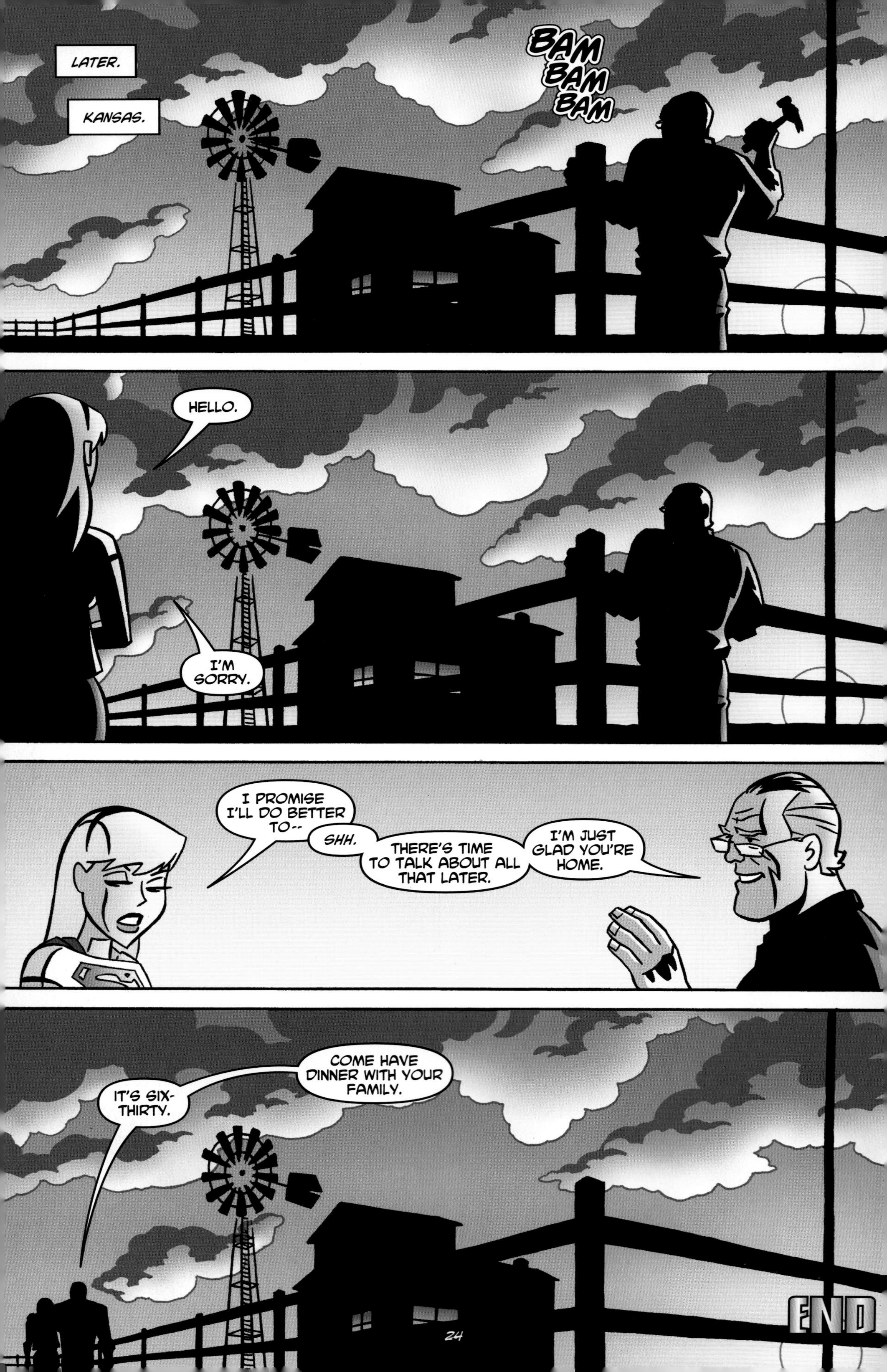
LATER.
KANSAS.
BAM BAM BAM
HELLO.
I'M SORRY.
I PROMISE I'LL DO BETTER TO--
SHH.
THERE'S TIME TO TALK ABOUT ALL THAT LATER.
I'M JUST GLAD YOU'RE HOME.
IT'S SIX-THIRTY.
COME HAVE DINNER WITH YOUR FAMILY.
END

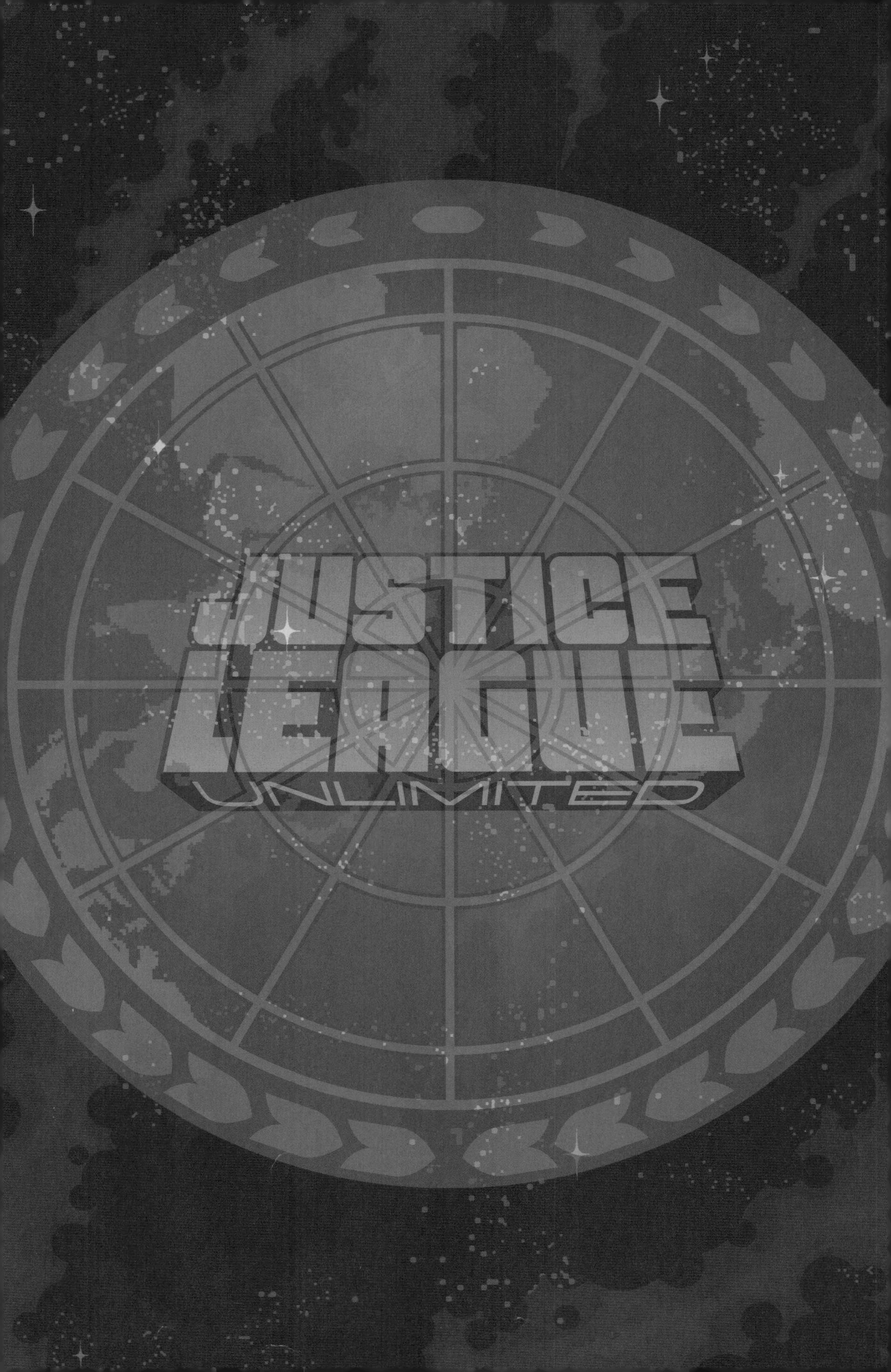
JUSTICE
LEAGUE
UNLIMITED

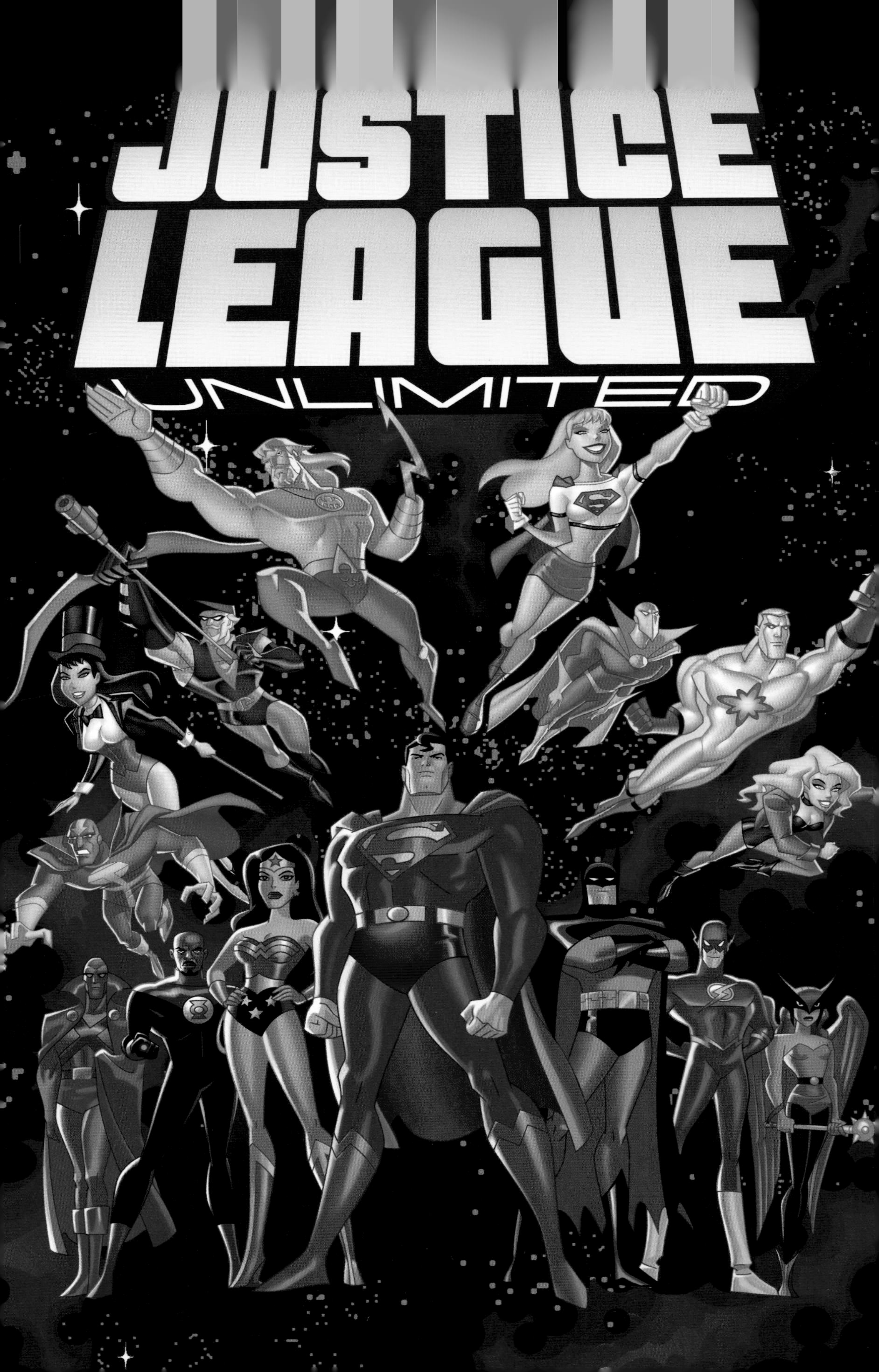
JUSTICE LEAGUE
UNLIMITED

JUSTICE LEAGUE UNLIMITED
MONITOR DUTY
JUSTICE LEAGUE UNLIMITED
IN THE DIMMING LIGHT
JUSTICE LEAGUE UNLIMITED
DARKSEID'S INFERNO!
JUSTICE LEAGUE UNLIMITED
WHO IS THE QUESTION?
JUSTICE LEAGUE UNLIMITED
DIVIDE AND CONQUER
JUSTICE LEAGUE UNLIMITED
POKER FACE
JUSTICE LEAGUE UNLIMITED
SMALL TIME
JUSTICE LEAGUE UNLIMITED
LOCAL HERO

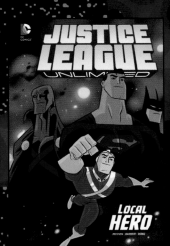

CREATORS

ADAM BEECHEN WRITER

Adam Beechen has written a variety of TV cartoons, including *Ben Ten: Alien Force, Teen Titans, Batman: The Brave and the Bold, The Batman* [for which he received an Emmy nomination], *Rugrats, The Wild Thornberrys, X-Men: Evolution,* and *Static Shock*, as well as the live-action series *Ned's Declassified School Survival Guide* and *The Famous Jett Jackson*. He is also the author of *Hench*, a graphic novel, and has scripted many comic books, including *Batgirl, Teen Titans, Robin,* and *Justice League Unlimited*. In addition Adam has written dozens of children's books, as well as an original young adult novel, *What I Did On My Hypergalactic Interstellar Summer Vacation*.

ETHAN BEAVERS ARTIST

Ethan Beaver is a professional comic book artist from Modesto, California. His best-known works for DC Comics include *Justice League Unlimited* and *Legion of Superheroes in the 31st Century*. He has also illustrated for other top publishers, including Marvel, Dark Horse, and Abrams.

WORD GLOSSARY

ancient (AYN-shuhnt)--very old, or belonging to a time from long ago

conquer (KONG-kur)--to defeat and take control of an enemy

destiny (DESS-tuh-nee)--your destiny is your fate or the future of your life

flank (FLANGK)--to guard or be at the side of something

prophecies (PROF-uh-seez)--predictions, or events fated to happen in the future

sired (SYE-urd)--fathered

synthesize (SIN-thuh-size)--to form or combine separate elements into a single entity

telepathic (tel-uh-PATH-ik)--communication between minds through thought alone

tyranny (TEER-uh-nee)--cruel or unjust exercise of power

ultimate (UHL-tuh-mit)--last or final, or greatest or best

whelp (WELP)--a disliked or unwanted young child

J.L.U. GLOSSARY

X-CANNON

A weapon created by Darkseid that is powerful enough to destroy nearly anything, living or not.

ELASTICITY

Elongated Man's body chemistry allows him to stretch to extreme lengths and twist himself into any imaginable position.

SUPER-STRENGTH

Supergirl and Superman possess super-strength. With this superpower, they can perform amazing feats and fight off fearsome foes.

VISUAL QUESTIONS & PROMPTS

1. What do you think J'onn's role was in the Justice League's fight with Darkseid's forces? Why?

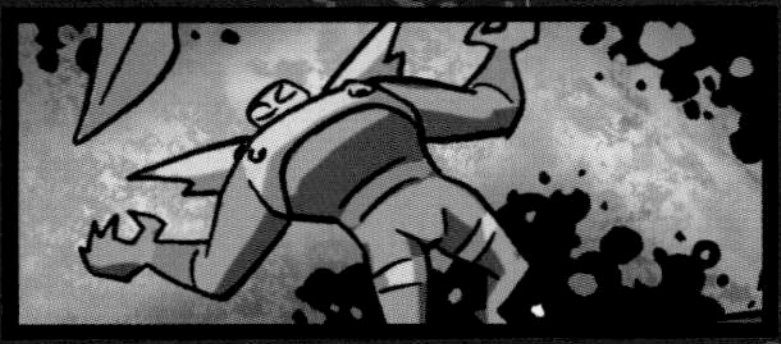

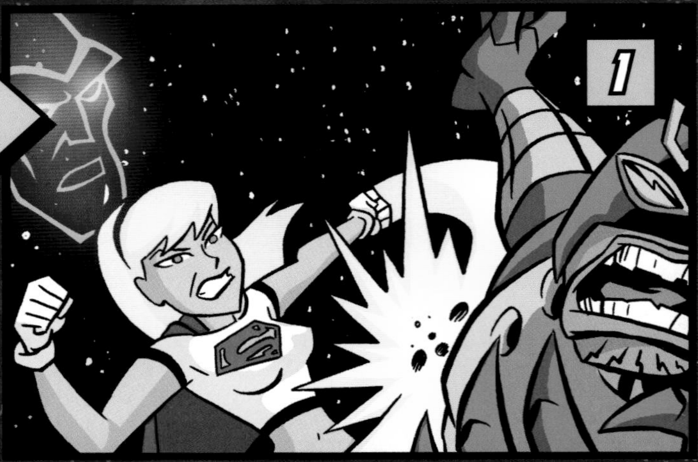
1

2. In the panel below, a strange symbol can be seen burning in Darkseid's eyes. Identify the other panels in this comic book where the symbol can be seen.

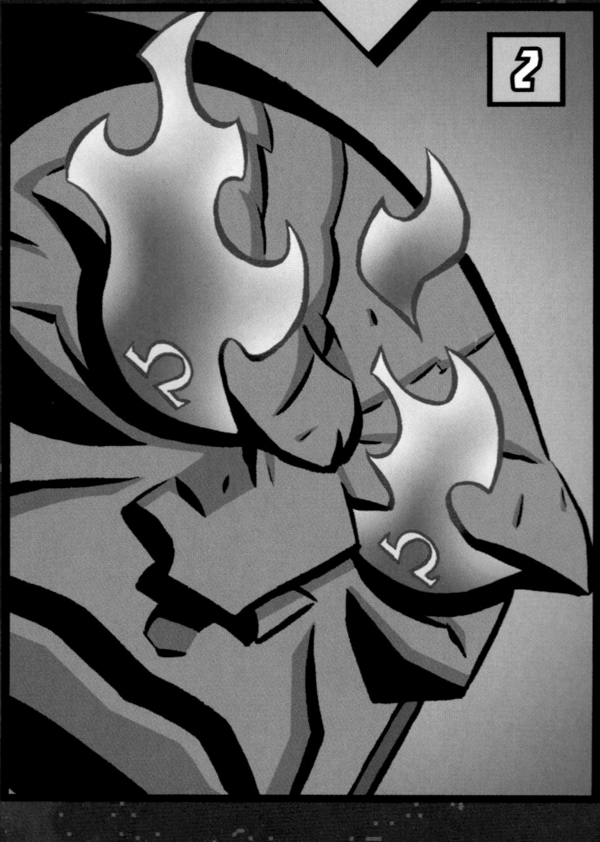
2

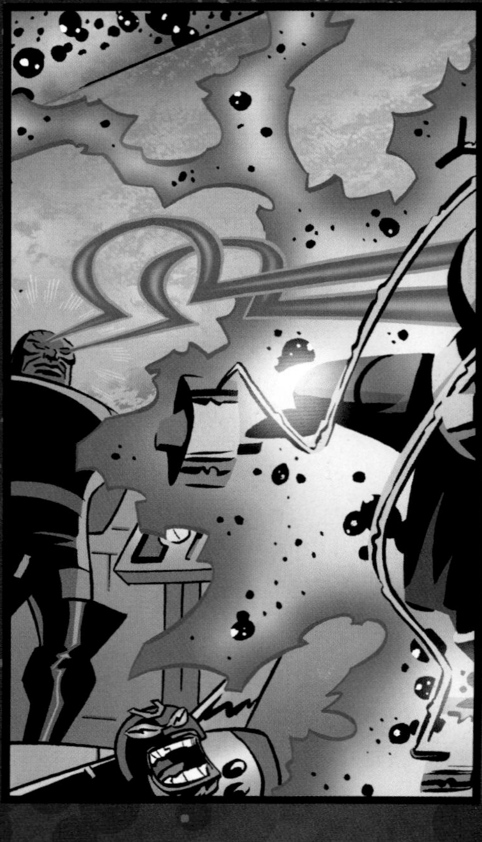

3. Why do the narration boxes in this panel have different colors and styles? Check the surrounding panels on page 9 for clues.

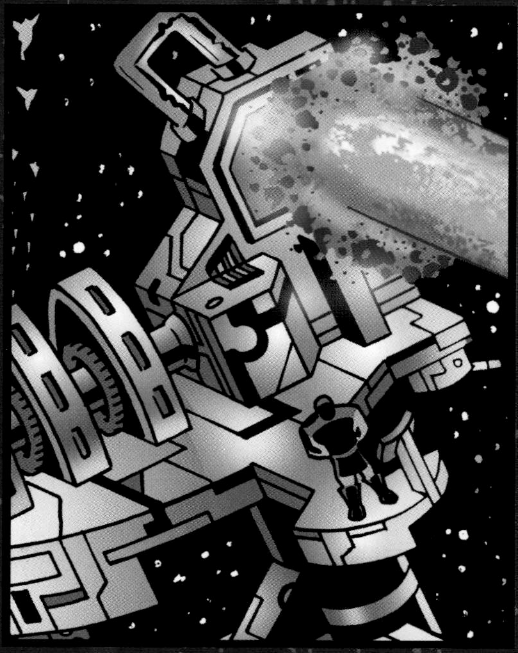

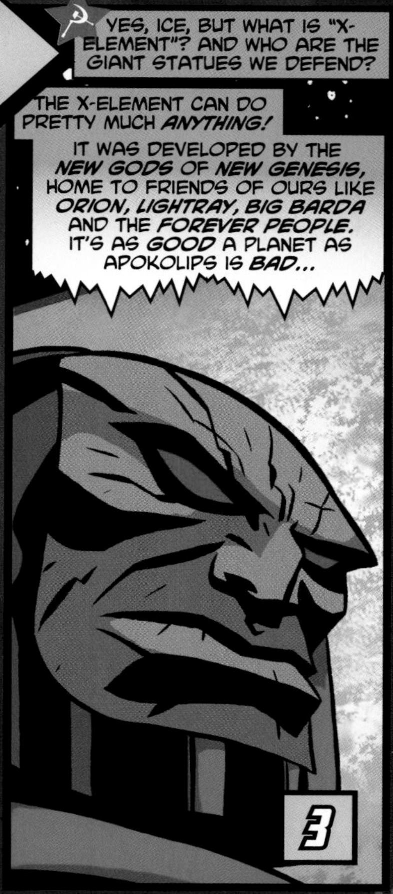
YES, ICE, BUT WHAT IS "X-ELEMENT"? AND WHO ARE THE GIANT STATUES WE DEFEND?
THE X-ELEMENT CAN DO PRETTY MUCH ANYTHING!
IT WAS DEVELOPED BY THE NEW GODS OF NEW GENESIS, HOME TO FRIENDS OF OURS LIKE ORION, LIGHTRAY, BIG BARDA AND THE FOREVER PEOPLE. IT'S AS GOOD A PLANET AS APOKOLIPS IS BAD...
3

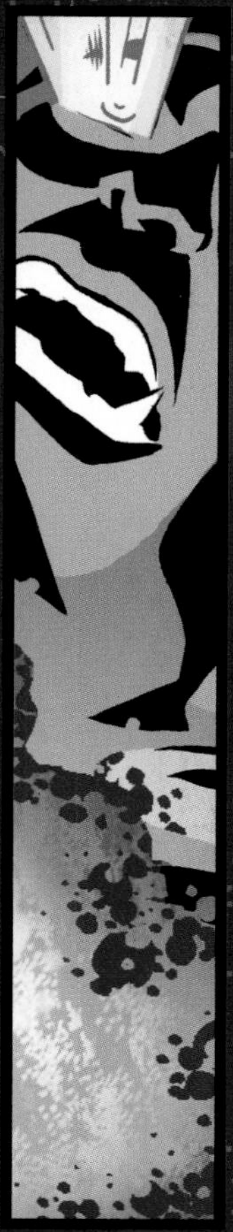

4. Based on her expression, how do you think Supergirl feels in each panel?

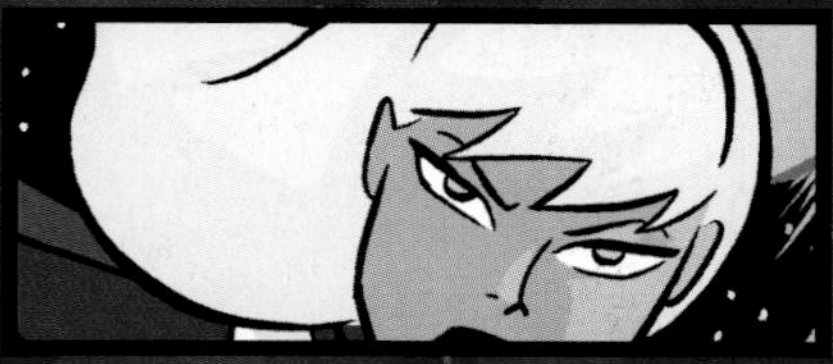

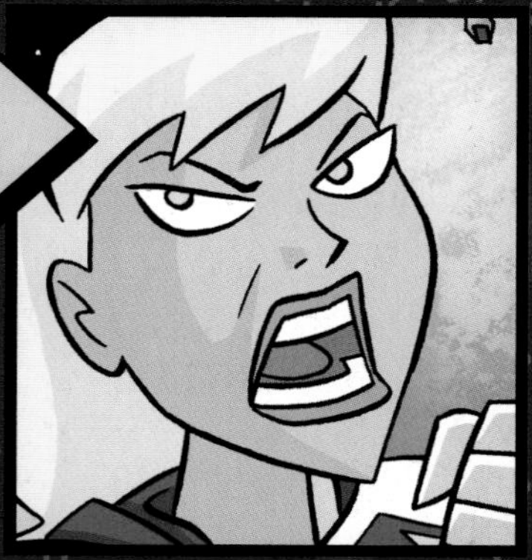

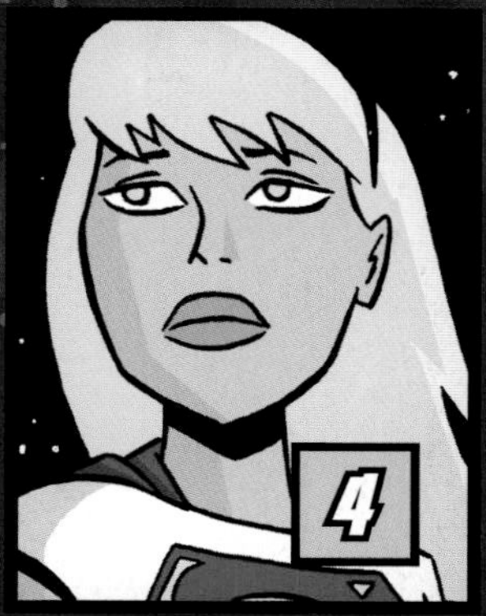
4

5. Why do you think this comic's creators chose to add an orange background to this panel? How does it make you feel compared to the surrounding panels on page 13?

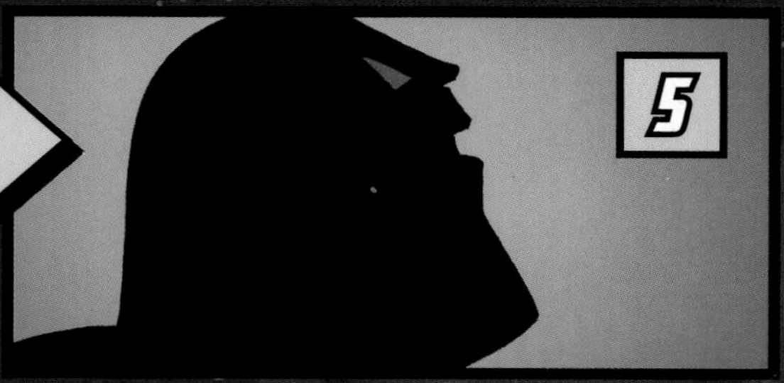
5

WANT EVEN MORE?

GO TO...

WWW.CAPSTONEKIDS.COM

Then find cool websites and more books like this one at *www.facthound.com.*

Just type in the BOOK ID:
9781434260437